A Place to Be

Jesse Falzoi writes with the authority of somebody who understands that sorrow and happiness can't exist without each other. Her characters are as smart as she is, and like all good writers, the risks she takes on the page mean big rewards for her readers. Count me as a fan.

Alexi Zentner, author of Copperhead, Touch, *and* The Lobster Kings

This is a gifted debut. Stories which are so light and confident in their presence we can only marvel at how deep they delve into the hearts of their characters.

Mike McCormack, author of Solar Bones

In this haunting collection, one of Jesse Falzoi's characters imagines the word "Wuthering" means "From all directions and never the one you anticipated." Using this definition, these are Wuthering stories, coming at life from many angles, each one full of surprise and illumination. Falzoi's characters thrum with yearning – for connection, for meaning, for a place to be, to belong. They will find a permanent home inside your heart.

Gayle Brandeis, author of The Art of Misdiagnosis

A Place to Be

Jesse Falzoi

Bridge House

British Library Cataloguing in Publication Data
A Record of this Publication is available from the British
Library

ISBN 978-1-907335-65-5

This edition published 2019 by Bridge House Publishing
Manchester, England

All Bridge House books are published on paper derived
from sustainable resources.

A person who has not been completely alienated, who has remained sensitive and able to feel, who has not lost the sense of dignity, who is not yet "for sale", who can still suffer over the suffering of others, who has not acquired fully the having mode of existence – briefly, a person who has remained a person and not become a thing – cannot help feeling lonely, powerless, isolated in present-day society.

Erich Fromm, The Art of Loving

Contents

A Place to Be

For Sabine

Come and be a lazy lout
Put up your feet and lie about
Come to Caputh and forget all the rest
including your papa, if you think it best.

Albert Einstein to his son Eduard, 1931

A year before we got divorced I read in a magazine that Einstein once had a cottage in Caputh, a picturesque village about fifty kilometres away from Berlin. I told my husband that I wanted to have a look at it and packed my overnight bag. Our children were eight and eleven that year – the third wasn't born yet – and I hadn't been travelling on my own for a very long time, so I felt strangely excited as I boarded the train, and it didn't leave me until I stepped into a small hotel, whose owner, Mrs. Schwarz, was too young to have met Einstein, I would have thought, but she smiled and said, "It was my mother's duty to keep the fireplaces running. I sometimes went with her."

I looked at my watch and since it was already seven o'clock I asked, "Is it possible to get something to eat?"

"It's usually only breakfast. But I can make you a sandwich."

After she'd shown me my room, which was small and stifling, with a smell and furniture that brought back GDR times, I went to the dining hall and sat down at the table next to the window. Here also the cheap veneer, the cacophony of patterns, and the plastic flowers in vases of a red that hurt my eyes made me feel like being on one of my few visits to our Eastern relatives again, where everything

8

and everybody looked pale, temporary, and tasteless. I sat down next to a window and only now noticed the woman at the table in the corner. She seemed to be totally absorbed in her writing.

Mrs. Schwarz brought me my sandwich. Then she went to the counter and opened a bottle of beer, which she carried to the other table, together with a glass. She looked at me and smiled. "How about you?"

"I'd like the same."

"Don't you two know each other?"

The woman looked up.

"How long is that street of yours?" Mrs. Schwarz laughed and said, "You must have bumped into each other before."

The woman smiled at me and I smiled at her too, and then she brought her gaze back to her letter. I still had the smile on my face, feeling ridiculous somehow, although it wasn't the first time that such encounters occurred in my life, on the contrary, but mostly they led to some kind of exchange, regarding which kindergarten one's kids went to or which school, and a list of places where one could have met before. I wasn't expecting – or longing for – a deeper conversation, but my notion of politeness demanded at least recognition of the fact that we were neighbours.

Mrs. Schwarz didn't seem to wonder though, probably her mind was already switching to after-hours, which she would spend behind the door she was heading to now. The place seemed very quiet suddenly, to such a degree that I could hear the fountain pen sliding over the paper. I realized that we were the only guests, although I couldn't say for sure then, but the moment Mrs. Schwarz had left, I felt as if the other woman and I were the only people on earth, and it wasn't a good feeling. I could have gone up to my room or taken the short walk to the hotel near the station, where the busy parking lot had suggested a busy dining hall as well, but it was dark outside and it had started snowing, so the only option seemed to go up once I had finished my sparse meal although it was hardly half past seven.

I took out my book for company. It was a novel a friend of mine had given me and I had made the mistake of not taking a look at it before I left home. From the very first page it turned out to be not only badly written but of a genre I usually avoided, mystery. I gave up after the third page and looked out of the window, which showed the other woman as clearly as a mirror. She wore a woollen cardigan, similar to the one I was wearing, her hair was approximately as long as mine, only a slightly bit darker. She didn't seem to care much about her looks – no nail polish, no lipstick, no particular thoughts about a hairdo – like me, and was wearing jeans and winter boots as well. I couldn't stop looking at her: the permanent smile, the way she gazed at the ceiling from time to time, as if in deep thought or lost in memories, the way she led the fountain pen over the paper, so tenderly, elegantly, conscious, and natural at the same time.

There were already several pages piled up next to the sheet she was using. It had to be a long letter. Or maybe she was writing a copy for herself. Or the pile was just a draft and only now she was writing the real thing. I finished my sandwich and got up; she looked at me and said, "It's a small world."

I nodded. Then, I waited for her to go back to her letter, but she didn't, so I said, "Do you come here often?"

She smiled. "Another beer for you too?"

Next to the fridge, there was a black-and-white photo of Einstein sitting in the sun, stretched out on an old-fashioned lounger. Beneath the photo a hand-written note: "The fairest thing we can experience is the mysterious." As a child I loved to read mystery stories; one of my favourite books was *Tom's Midnight Garden*. I loved the thought that one could escape this world and that there was another world hidden somewhere, a place to be, where one felt safe and loved and accepted.

The other woman brought both bottles to her table and said, "Have a seat."

"You seem pretty busy."

She shoved the sheets to the side. "I could use a break."

We quickly covered the part that I'd expected when we were introduced to each other, and then she said, "Aren't you curious?"

"What?"

"I have a baby at home, I'm married like you, and I'm spending the night in a run-down hotel out of town, writing a never-ending letter." She picked up the pile and turned it around. "Mi amor," she read. "A love letter obviously."

A grey cat walked into the room. It stopped, looked me straight in the eye. The other woman smiled. "I could feel that you were observing me. But it's okay. I would have done the same."

"That's a nice fountain pen," I said.

She laid it in front of me. It was a Montblanc. "Write something." She passed me a page of her paper, which was delicate and solid at the same time; no doubt she had tried out how many pages would fit into an envelope and chosen this paper even though it probably was the most expensive. "My grandfather gave it to me before he died. He was in the SS. He wasn't big there, just one of the hundreds and thousands of desk criminals, but his signature caused a lot of sorrow. He kept it hidden in his desk all those years, looking for ways to make amends, and when he knew that his time was running up, he gave it to me. I had to promise that I would only use it in the name of love."

11

I carefully removed the cap. The nib was made of gold. Beneath the beautiful carving there was the date. 1938. "That's nice," I said.

She bit on her lower lip and after a while she said, "He was so gentle. He had such a friendly, warm voice. He read me books, he made me listen to his favourite records, he showed me how to carve wooden boats,. I once hid a shoe box with fifty snails under my bed – I'd numbered them! – and they crawled out while I was sleeping and the next day, they were all over the walls and the ceiling. My grandfather had to paint the whole room, and yet, he only laughed." She smiled. "Try it."

"Okay," I said, holding the fountain pen above the paper. My hand was shaking. Nothing important came to my mind. "I guess we all can be really good and really bad." The other woman frowned. "I don't want to know what I am capable of doing."

I looked around for inspiration and then just copied the lettering on our beer bottles, *Radeberger*. I closed the pen and returned it to her.

"I have the feeling that he's guiding my hand," she said. "It's silly, I know. Usually I have a very bad handwriting. I can't read it myself. That's why I don't feel comfortable writing something in long-hand. But with my grandpa's pen it feels so natural. As if I had been born with it."

"You should use it more often then."

"It isn't meant for anything else." She reached into her bag and produced a small notepad. "Look here," she said. "This is the way I usually write."

Her shopping list was hardly decipherable. Unsteady, scratchy, with neither rhythm nor pattern, as if she was perpetually asking herself in which direction she should go. "Would you even believe that it was one and the same person?" She opened and closed the pen, as if to check that the cap still fitted and then she said, "There is a World Fountain Pen Day, did you know? It's on the first Friday of November."

"Well," I said, reaching for my beer. "I don't want to keep you from finishing." I tried to get up but the cat had fallen asleep on my lap. I didn't dare push it away.

The other woman said, "Don't you want to know whom I'm writing it to?"

Something in her eyes disturbed me. I felt that it was wiser to go up to my room. I was hoping for a television set, be it an old one with only two or three channels. Tomorrow I would ask Mrs. Schwarz if she had books here, surely some of the guests had left one now and then. In the GDR, people read a lot. They had cheap editions of classics that could be bought everywhere. Books were special if they were forbidden, and yet, affordable for everyone, so it happened quite often then that people just left them behind for the next reader.

"I'm leaking," the other woman said, touching her right breast.

"There must be somebody missing you badly."

"Did you breastfeed?"

"Yes." I always had small breasts. It didn't bother me once that typical teenage competition phase was over, and yet, I'd felt surprisingly attractive as a young mother and started wearing tight sweaters to expose my new abundance.

"She only remembers when I'm around." The other woman laughed. "You should see that look on her face the moment I'm opening the front door."

I smiled. "I perfectly remember that look." When I finally decided to call it quits, I had to go on a holiday. I felt relieved, and yet, it made me sad to know that from now on all they needed they could get from their father as well.

13

"Do you speak Spanish?"

I shook my head.

"I would have liked to have your opinion."

"My opinion?" The disquieting wallpaper made it hard to focus on her face. I was distracted by uncountable circles of all sizes that looked like bracelets, not the thick ones, but the ones you wear by the dozen, like Hindu brides do. My daughter had recently shown up with such bracelets, driving everybody insane with the constant ding-a-ling; just looking at the wallpaper brought that horrible noise back to me.

"It sounds terribly romantic sometimes," the other woman said. "The whole thing is maybe overdone."

"But I don't even know him."

"You don't know me either." She reached for the first page and browsed over it. "Like a teenager really. Well, aren't we all a bit silly when we're in love?"

I shrugged.

"Why did you do that?" she said and I said, "What?"

She bent forward. "Have you never been in love?"

"Of course." I took out my cell to check the time. It was nearly eight o'clock. The kids would be in bed now and my husband stretched out on the sofa, watching one of the TV-series he got addicted to lately. He'd tried to get me interested but didn't feel like going back to the beginning, and I found it difficult to start in the middle of things. Now that we had subscribed to a pay channel he was glued to the screen every evening.

"Here, for example, I'm writing about our trip to Hamburg." She pointed at a paragraph on the third page. "That was last year, when I was near my due date. They all took him for the father. I pretended to feel embarrassed, but it felt kind of nice." She put her hand on her now flat belly. "He held his hand like this. He wanted to feel her kicking."

14

The cat began to purr. Maybe cats purr when they dream of something nice. Was it a dream that caused it or my hand that had begun to caress its back against my will? I continued caressing the soft grey fur; I was careful of course, but surely the cat would have enough of it soon and then finally jump to the floor again, hopefully keeping the claws inside.

"I come here once a month," the woman said. "I leave Friday afternoon and return home the next morning."

I looked up. "What do you say to your husband?"

"He understands that I need my time out. He's very good with the kids. I totally trust him."

I grinned. "Your time out, eh?"

"Strictly speaking, I'm not cheating on him." She looked at the letter again. "We never kissed or had sex or even considered it. Well, we didn't out in the open. And thoughts are free, aren't they?"

"If my husband wrote love letters to somebody else, I would feel betrayed," I said.

"How do you know that he doesn't?" she said.

I took a sip from my beer. "I don't think that this is our problem."

"What *is* your problem?"

The cat suddenly twitched and jumped off my lap. I felt naked all of a sudden, as if the wind had lifted my skirt. I put my bottle down and said, "Where's the bathroom?"

She pointed at the door next to the bar. With the hand that would affectionately reach out for two men, to one in a concrete sense, to the other in an abstract. "Over there."

The key was missing. Our daughter locked herself in the bathroom at the age of three and couldn't get out again, so we had to break the door. Maybe something like this happened here too. But there was a window, and we were on ground floor. They must have lost it.

15

When I returned, I smiled and said, "Why did you let that opportunity pass?"

She curled her lip. It made her look much younger. "How do you know that it was one for him as well?"

I looked at the pile again. At her neat handwriting. At the extensive curves and lines that cried out to be answered, that spoke of passion even to me who didn't understand a word. "You wouldn't write such a letter to somebody who didn't love you back."

She rolled up her sleeves. Around her left wrist, she had a bracelet that resembled the ones my daughter wore, but hers most probably was of pure gold, and it didn't make a noise, of course not, it couldn't hit against other ones. She cupped her hand around it and said, "Are you only able to love if it's returned?"

"It would be stupid to long for something you can't have anyway."

She got up to exchange our empty bottles with full ones. "So you never loved somebody who didn't love you?" she said when she sat down again.

The beep of an incoming text message came out of my bag. It was from my husband. I turned the phone off without opening it. "I've been married for such a long time. I don't remember."

"When you were young? You must have been in and out of love when you were young." She giggled. "I was."

I put my hand around the ice-cold bottle. I held it against my hot cheeks. The heating bill had to be enormous. But maybe Mrs. Schwarz was beyond caring. Maybe, at one point, when it's clear that your business won't make it much longer, you decide to give it one last good time. You stop worrying and you stop calculating and you just let go – and when the end is there, you think about these last weeks and days, and not the horrible ones you had, when you desperately tried to keep things running.

"She turned the heating up for us. She doesn't have many guests anymore." The other woman went out the same door Mrs. Schwarz had vanished behind, and when she came back, she said, "It will cool down soon."

Only now I realized that the circles formed a gigantic maze, one that would trap you and never let you get out again. "There were maybe two," I said. "A long time ago. But as soon as I understood that they were not interested I got out of it."

She snapped her fingers. "Like this?"

"Well..."

"You were able to turn it off, like a switch?"

I reached for my beer. I drank. I put it down again, and I said, "I don't remember."

"I wish I were able to do that." She looked down at her letter, and then she said, "I know that it's unfair. I know that I'm dishonest. I wasn't expecting it, see?" She looked me in the eye, and again I felt very uncomfortable and wished I could just get up and leave, and of course, nobody was forcing me to stay; even the cat wasn't keeping me here anymore; I could always pretend that I had a headache or that I was tired if I feared to be judged for impoliteness, and if I met her on the street – which most probably wouldn't happen, it hadn't happened in the fifteen years we'd been living there – I could just look the other way or pretend that I was busy with my phone; I could get it out now and read my husband's message and tell her that I needed to call home, that an emergency had happened with the kids. I could bring up a thousand excuses.

"I didn't realize then. Or maybe I did and pushed it away. I'd just become pregnant with my third child. To fall in love was really the last thing I expected and wished for."

17

She looked down at her letter again, which her hand was caressing now, and she stayed silent for a while. Then she raised her head and said, "Suddenly, I became aware of myself in the morning, when I dressed, when I washed my face, when I took breakfast. I looked at myself in the mirror, realizing that it was the woman he saw when he was looking at me. Things I was doing without thinking became important, no, that's not the right word, not important, but significant, I suddenly *realized* that I was doing them, as if there was somebody else by my side. I mean, apart from the ones who actually were there." Her hand was still caressing the letter. "He is from Costa Rica, did I tell you?"

I shook my head.

"He came to Germany five years ago. His grandfather or great-grandfather was German. He didn't speak it though." She smiled. "He still doesn't speak it well."

I went to the fridge and took out two new bottles. There was no Radeberger anymore, just Beck's. As I opened the first bottle my glance fell on the windows. The snow had been piling up on the sill. And it continued coming down the size of cotton balls. "Maybe you can't get home tomorrow," I said.

She started to peel off the beer's label. "It will stop, you'll see." She raised her bottle. "I hope I'm not keeping you from, I don't know, something important."

"No," I said.

All of a sudden, a fountain of beer foam flowed out of her bottle. "So we came…"

"Watch out," I said.

She looked at the bottle and then onto her letter. "Oh," she said.

I pressed my sleeve onto the sheet. "Pure cotton. It will soak it up." After a while, I removed my wrist. "See, just let it dry for a bit."

She still looked at the letter dumbfounded. Then, she bundled up all the sheets and started to rip them apart. "You're right. This has to stop."

"No," I cried out. "Please." I reached for her hands and said, "Why don't you read it to me?"

She frowned. "You said you don't speak Spanish."

"Read it to me anyway." I let go of her hands and smiled. "Please."

She browsed over the pages again and said, "You must think that I'm totally nuts."

"Please," I said. "I really would like to hear it."

She straightened the pages, touching the spot where she had ripped them, as if she could undo it that way, and then she cleared her throat and began to read. I didn't understand a word, and yet, I understood everything. I could see them sitting on the fresh spring grass, somewhere in a park, in the morning, when there wouldn't be many people, just a jogger now and then. Or next to a lake, watching the row boats gliding by. Or at the beach, with their naked feet buried in the sand, listening to the burble of the hardly noticeable waves, and from time to time one of them would say something and the other would listen and reply, but only if necessary. They didn't touch, not once, and yet, I'd never seen two people so close to each other.

"That's it," she eventually said.

I opened my eyes, squinted against the artificial light, the unsettling wallpaper.

"He went back to Costa Rica when he was diagnosed with multiple sclerosis." She folded the sheets and put them into an envelope, which was made from the same paper. "He owns a piece of land on the coast." She reached into her bag and produced a crumpled clipping: a hidden beach with white sand and palm trees. No people. One of the palm trees was right next to the sea, with its branches bending toward

19

it, as if the leaves wanted to drink from the turquoise water. Hundreds of years ago, someone must have steered a ship toward the coast, someone must have been overthrown by the beauty. Why else come up with that name?

"If he was going to die, he said, he wanted it to happen there."

I said, "It isn't always lethal, I think."

She reached for her fountain pen and wrote his name: Fabián Díaz, and beneath it, the address: Lugar lleno de amor, Santa Teresa, Costa Rica.

"Is that where he lives now?" I asked.

"Yes," she said, leaning the envelope against a flower pot on the window sill.

I leaned forward, whispered, "Why didn't you go with him?"

She got up, took down the framed photograph of Einstein, put it on the table. "Nobody can understand me. People don't believe in the mysterious. If something isn't concrete they don't think that it can affect you." She smiled. "My husband and I came here ten years ago. I never forgot that photo. I knew that Einstein would understand." She stopped smiling. Again she made this thing with her lip that made her look so much younger. Then she said, "Have you been to the cottage?"

"No."

"Get your coat."

I followed her out of the still overheated dining hall, through the deserted reception area, out into the cold. The snow was hitting me in the face like pebbles. I couldn't see anything.

She reached for my arm and held onto it. "Close your eyes," she said, "I'm guiding you."

A couple of minutes later we reached the cottage. I had seen photographs on the internet.

It was kind of a museum nowadays. I couldn't imagine

20

people leaving it unlocked, but she didn't take out a key but just pushed the door and it opened. "The lights don't work in winter," she said. "Just sit down here."

I reached out and felt a lounger. "Is it the one from the photo?" I asked.

"Yes," she said. "I'll see if there's wood. A fire would be nice, wouldn't it?"

She let go of my arm and the feeling of sudden nakedness returned. "I'm over here," she said. "There's plenty of wood. It won't take long."

I heard her piling up logs and then I saw her holding a lighter to them. The flame was small at first but after a while the whole fireplace became visible and the room emerged out of the darkness. There was a desk and a chair and a bookshelf that was empty except for a small radio that looked too modern even though it was far from being new.

She sat down at the desk. "Imagine him sitting here. With his head full of all these crazy ideas."

"I never understood any of it," I said.

"You don't have to." She turned around and said, "Actually there are a lot of things you won't understand if you try to understand them."

"When you return home," I began. Then I stopped.

"Yes?" she said.

"Isn't it hard?"

"It helps me to know that there's a second home where everything I do is okay."

The boy in the novel had such a home. As soon as the clock struck thirteen, he would go to a beautiful garden to see this girl from the past, who, unlike him, quickly grew older and eventually married a man her age. The night before the boy was leaving, he wanted to go the garden one last time, but instead he crashed into a set of rubbish bins.

"You're thinking that the life you have is the only one

you can have," the other woman said. "How easily it could be the complete opposite. I am here now sitting with you but how easily could I be somewhere else."

"In Costa Rica?"

She laughed. "Where would your second home be?"

"Can't think of one."

She got up and kneeled next to me. "One good thing about this second home is that time's slower over there. People won't even notice that you've been away." She got up and turned on the radio. The news anchor's voice was so warm and tender that the massacre at a secondary school in Bremen seemed like a fairytale that surely would have a good ending. Then, the radio host took over and announced "Your Song".

"I can't stand him," I said.

"He's terribly schmaltzy," she said.

"Terribly," I said.

She put her hands around my waist and we danced. We danced until the last schmaltzy tone faded away and then let go off each other. She chuckled. "I have to go to the bathroom."

"We should go back," I said. "It must be very late."

"What did I just say about time?"

The fire had gone out; it was cold and dark again. Only the little red lamp of the radio was still shining. After a while it went out too and with it the music. I felt my way along the wall to find the door through which she had vanished but there was only the one leading outside. She must have gone back to the hotel. Maybe that's what she meant when she said that she needed to go to the bathroom. Maybe there wasn't one here. It was still snowing but by now the storm had stopped and I could see the hotel down the road.

I silently opened the front door and walked past the reception desk and then to the dining hall. Mrs. Schwarz must have cleared up after us. The framed picture was back on the wall and our glasses, the empty bottles, even the plate, were gone. I went to the bathroom. It was locked. I knocked at the door. "Are you in there?" I whispered. Only now I realized that I didn't know her name. I waited for a couple of minutes and then I returned to the dining hall where the cat was lying on my chair again, softly purring.

Upstairs I turned my phone on again. It wasn't even nine o'clock. The display reminded me of my husband's unread message, but I couldn't bring myself to open it. I switched off the light and soon fell asleep, but two hours later I woke up again and lay awake until dawn, asking myself why I hadn't knocked at the other doors to make sure that she had returned too.

The next morning I took breakfast at the table where we'd been sitting the night before and on my seat, I found a crumpled page. It was the paper she'd been using but there were no words, just this drawing.

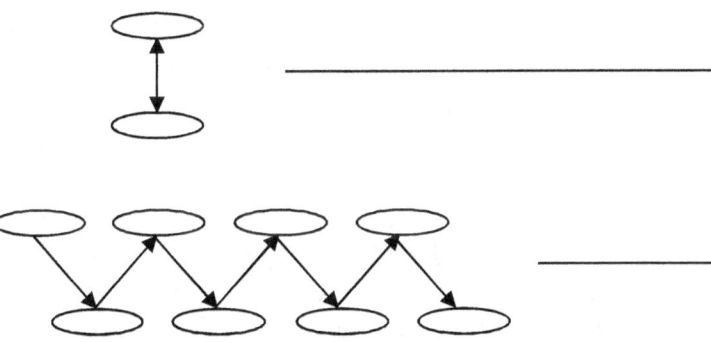

I could hardly keep my eyes open and every move I made was painfully slow and uncoordinated, so I decided to leave. I longed to sleep in my own bed and I longed to look at white walls. When I paid I asked Mrs. Schwarz if the other woman had gone, but she just looked at me frowning. I laughed. "We drank all your Radeberger."

Now she laughed too. "If there's one thing that I have plenty of it's beer."

"Did Einstein write it? On that photograph that shows him on the lounger?"

"Oh that?" She handed me my bill that still itemized marks instead of euros. "I honestly don't know. Didn't you want to go to the cottage? You know that it's closed in winter, don't you? But it's worth having a look at it anyway. If you don't mind walking a bit. It's on the other side of the village." She reached under the counter and showed me a map. "Look. You just walk past the station and after about ten minutes you'll find it to your right. But maybe you want to come back in summer when it's open for visitors." The ringing of the telephone interrupted her. She picked up the receiver. "Goldener Anker. How can I help you?" She listened for a while, then covered the earpiece with her hand and whispered to me, "Is there anything else I can do for you?"

I shook my head, shouldered my overnight bag, and went outside. It had stopped snowing and the streets were cleared. The train came hardly five minutes after I'd arrived at the tiny station, and by the time I found a seat, Einstein's village was out of sight. There were merely vast brownish fields, with a few white dots here and there, a deserted, depressing landscape. I closed my eyes and when I opened them again a man around my age, who seemed out of place in his elegant business clothes, was sitting opposite me, crying silently. I quickly closed my eyes again and kept them closed until I reached my destination.

My husband didn't turn his gaze from the screen when I looked into the living room, not even in surprise, although

24

I was back much earlier than we both had thought. There was a man standing on a porch, with a glass of whisky in one hand and a cigarette in the other. Some dramatic music told me that it had to be a turning point in his life. Then the credits began and my husband said, "How was it?"

"Einstein's cottage? It's closed in winter." I went to the kitchen and checked the fridge for food but grabbed the last beer instead and drank it sitting on the window sill.

It was a Radeberger.

With my index finger I followed the elegant curves on the label.

The longing handwriting, reaching out, craving to be loved back.

Say to Yourself

Do not cancel the dinner appointment with your friends. You promised to cook coq au vin, go shopping and think about which salad to serve it with. Leave it to Stan to choose the wine. Leave important decisions to him. Choosing the wine is an important decision. Propose to prepare tiramisu for dessert. Say: "Dinner comes with a dessert." Say it with a rolling "R": "I want tiramisu."

Tell Stan that Gerry called in the afternoon. Say: "He'll bring somebody." Try to figure out how long he hasn't dated anybody. Wink at Stan and say: "Wouldn't it be nice for our Gerry?"

Say: "It's a good thing. Us all having dinner together again."

Try to think of something else for a while. The doctor said that you can't do anything right now. The doctor said that there is no immediate danger anymore. Finally, you'd be able to say: "My daughter nearly died." Or even better: "Our daughter nearly died."

Coq au vin and tiramisu. It's high time that you both got something to eat.

Open the window. The neighbours are going to complain because the yard will echo every word back, but soon you will be too drunk to care.

"You're allowed to throw a party once a year," Gerry says, smiling at you. His arm self-confidently resting around Ulrike's shoulders. She's got dark brown hair that reaches her hips. The flames of the candles flicker up and down on them.

Pretend to like the food. Say: "Is it good?" Say: "I was starving." Ask Stan for more to make him believe you. Give him the opportunity to show that he functions.

Smile.

Don't say that your daughter is in hospital. You might not be able to stop if you once bring it up. The doctor said that you need a break. Until yesterday one of you slept on the cot next to the hospital bed. A month ago you invited your friends to dinner. Gerry's call to announce that he would bring somebody reminded you. Now he says, "How about throwing a party again?"

Say: "We are too old for parties." Say: "The only thing we get now are dinners for couples."

"Food is the new sex," Gerry says.

The other ones are Nils and Sarah; you expected her successor after the usual two-year-period, but still it's Sarah. "I thought we were immortal," Nils says.

You talk about the goal keeper who threw himself in front of a train. "That may be the fear of failing," Sarah says. "Perhaps they want to show the pressure on people nowadays."

Light a cigarette. It's okay that you started again. You'll quit again. When things get back to normal. Read aloud what's written on the package: "Smoking is highly addictive. Do not even start it." Laugh along as the others laugh. Don't think of your daughter. Don't think of her holding her nose. Don't think of what she would think of you smoking in the apartment.

"Pressure?" Gerry says, "What kind of pressure?"

You've been sitting in the kitchen since eight, drinking. First, you've been eating, but now you only fill glasses and clear them again. The tiramisu is still in the fridge. You're waiting for a good moment to say, "Who wants tiramisu?"

Say to yourself: A hospital full of doctors. Nothing could be safer.

"It's not as simple as that," Ulrike says.

Sarah says, "You're right. It's disgusting, all this bullshit coming from the media at the moment."

27

Smile at her. Show her that you like her. Stan told you that Nils had a few dates with the new editing assistant, but up to now he hasn't stayed overnight. Stan went back to work yesterday. Because the doctor said that they should get back to their routine. Because the doctor said that the worst is over. Smile at Stan. Show him that he's hanging in bravely. Show him that it's okay if he drinks too much.

"I feel sorry for the wife," Sarah says. "For the family."

Stan puts his hand onto your forearm. "Can you open another one, please?"

There is a line of empty bottles on the window sill. The bowl out of which you usually eat your cereals serves as an ashtray now. It's overflowing.

Don't feel guilty. Your daughter wouldn't get better if you smoked and drank less. It wouldn't keep her from having her foot amputated. Say to yourself: Nothing is lost right now. Say to yourself: The doctor keeps talking about a 20% chance that they would be able to save it. Say to yourself: Better footless than dead. Do not say to yourself: My daughter has just turned fifteen.

"My ex-husband suffered from depression too," Ulrike says. "I had a hard time trying to accept that I couldn't help him." She has the habit of twirling strands of her hair around her index finger. "And that I even made it worse with my compassion," she continues.

Gerry puts his hand on her thigh. "Compassion is bad."

Say: "Compassion is always bad." Take a sip of your wine and say: "How long have you been with him?"

"Five years," Ulrike says. "I wouldn't have survived without Gerry."

Put bowls with chips and peanuts onto the table. Clear the cereal bowl that you've been using as an ashtray and place it far away from the other bowls to prevent everybody from tapping the ash off their cigarettes into the chips.

28

Ash is sterile.

Nils puts one nut after the other into his mouth while staring at Ulrike. Sarah leans her head on his shoulder, but he doesn't seem to realize. Say to yourself: Sarah isn't happy. Say to yourself: Nils isn't happy. Say to yourself: Someday this evening will just be a memory.

The doctor said, "You need some downtime." Down. Time. It's okay if you feel like taking words apart. It's okay that everything the others are saying feels like a trap. Put "down" and "time" together again. See? It doesn't hurt anymore.

Fill the glasses. Say: "What shall we drink to?"

"Ulrike has been through hard times," Gerry says, biting into a chip like a rabbit. Think of the rabbit that you had as a child. Consider whether it ate chips. Think of stroking the silver grey fur. Think of its racing heart after you caught it. Do not think about the morning when you lifted the little wooden house your father had built. When you saw the stiff corpse.

Offer more wine to your guests. Say: "Anyone care for dessert?" Say: "Anyone care for tiramisu?" Say it with a rolling "R". Laugh, when you translate: "Lift-Me-Up."

Listen, when Gerry's New Girl says something. Listen, when she says, "We thought that he had taken it quite well, but then he started to spy on me. And to write all these mails. That he would always love me. That he couldn't live without me. He thought he was some kind of Heathcliff, with me being Cathy, like in Charlotte Brontë's novel…"

"Emily," says Stan.

"He continually threatened to kill himself. And her, too," Gerry says.

Stan nods. Stan is still doing well. Stan says, "A typical case of borderline. They just didn't have a name for it back then."

Think of your trip to Haworth before your final year of study. Think of the parsonage. Think of the plain grey dress in the display cabinet, of your astonishment when you realized how small the owner must have been.

Try to imagine Charlotte and Emily walking through the moors. The heels of their lace-up shoes sinking into the mud. The seams of their dresses getting heavier. The moist air drenching the cloth. The wind coming from all directions. *Wuthering*. When you asked locals for the meaning they shrugged their shoulders, as if they didn't know it either. But you were sure that they did.

If somebody asked you, you would say: From all directions and never the one you anticipated.

Nils says, "All the Young Writers on Laudanum."

Sarah says, "What?"

Try to imagine Cathy and Heathcliff leaning against the wind. Coming from all directions. The moist air drenching the cloth. Put your hand on Stan's upper leg. Feel the cloth. It is dry.

"Just a book," Stan says.

Think of the tearoom in Yorkshire. Think of the student from Leeds. Who talked to you in German. The student of German studies who asked you for your address. You didn't anticipate then that he would really show up. You didn't anticipate then where this would lead to.

The student of German studies. Sitting opposite to you now. With your hand on his upper leg. With a daughter whose small face is lying on the white hospital pillow.

Better footless than dead.

Laugh when your ring gets caught in your daughter's cardigan. Ignore Stan's look as you want to bring it to the bathroom where the washing machine is nearly full.

"Leave it," he says.

Focus on Ulrike. On her straight composure. Look at

her bosom, her chin, her mouth, her eyes, and say: "What happened to your ex?"

"He committed suicide," she says. "I still find it difficult to accept, but Gerry is a big help."

Nils wipes the crumbs of the peanuts and the chips onto his plate. "Did you know him?"

"He was at Verena's party, don't you remember?" Gerry says, looking at Ulrike as if to ask for her permission. "His name was Richard. Tall guy, blond curls."

Stan says, "Him?"

You remember, of course. Him touching your shoulder. Leaving his hand there while talking to you. You felt his warm fingers through the tissue of your blouse. When he left to get a beer you had to put on your cardigan. Say to yourself: There was nothing I could do. Say to yourself: I can't save people who want to die.

Stan looks at you.

Say: "Did I meet him?"

Gerry says, grinning, "I'd say so."

Say, grinning: "Alzheimer's."

Sarah wants to support you. Her laughter crushes into the yard and back into the kitchen. Then she looks at Gerry. "And since when are you two…?"

"Together?" Gerry says, "As in couple-language?"

Ulrike takes a packet of Gauloises out of her bag. "Are we together?"

Gerry runs his fingers through her hair. He holds it to the side and lights her cigarette.

Sarah says, "Isn't it strange what people are willing to do out of love?"

Say to yourself: She's sleeping. Repeat: She's sleeping. Say to yourself: There's nothing safer than a hospital. Say to yourself: If something went wrong your mobile would ring. Say to yourself: If something went wrong your display would show it. Take the word apart: Dis. Play. Consider whether "dis" is a negative prefix. Put the word together again.

Gerry looks at Sarah. "What the fuck are you talking about?"

Sarah looks at you, expecting your support. "Didn't he kill himself out of love?"

"This is stupid," Nils says.

Twirling a strand of hair around her index finger, Ulrike says, "He did love me, though."

"He's been putting you through hell." Gerry says, "How can you even talk about love here?"

Nils says, "Nobody knows what love is."

Collect the cigarette butts that fell out of the cereal bowl you use as an ashtray. Put them into saran wrap before throwing them into the waste bin. Saran wrap takes the reek away. With saran wrap your daughter won't notice. Do not look at Stan. Say to yourself: Stan will manage. Say to yourself: The worst is over. Say to yourself: There is your husband, here are you and in a few days there will be your daughter, sitting where Sarah is Now sitting, Now saying, "I do know what love is."

Say: "You feel love. And when it's gone, it's better to go, too." Look out of the window. Count the empty bottles. Try to imagine yourself taking them down the stairs tomorrow and throwing them into the container. The glass breaking.

When your cell rings, let Stan answer the call. Wait until he puts it back onto the table. Wait until he says: "Her heart didn't make it."

Say to yourself: Someday this evening will just be a memory.

When the Curtain Closes

It happened on a Tuesday night. The lights went off and the radio stopped and the flame beneath the pot died down. "This time they will be a bit too al dente, I'm afraid," Judith said.

Her twelve-year-old daughter stood up and felt her way to the fuse box. Her son, who had turned nine a month ago, ran into his room to get the Ghostbusters kit. Judith looked out the window, at the moonless night, at the sky that was not grey anymore but black, then her son returned and aimed the gun at the wall where a smiling ghost was dancing.

"Gotcha," he shouted.

"Give me that." Judith grabbed the pistol and the plastic skull and turned both off. "We'll need the batteries."

When her daughter returned she told her to get the candle stand from the living room.

"The fuses are okay," her daughter said. "It must be something else." She stepped up to the window. "It's a blackout, right? Oh my God."

"Don't worry. It used to happen all the time when we first moved here." Judith smiled. "That was before you were born. After the wall came down they had to renew everything. They turned off the gas one day, on another electricity or water. But in the end, they turned everything on again."

She checked the lighters. One was nearly empty and the other half full. They had twenty-three tea lights and a pile of used and unused candles of all sizes. "A candlelight dinner," she turned around and smiled. "Isn't it nice?"

They sat down to eat. They were lucky. The sauce had been ready for a while and was still hot. Her son had filled their glasses with tap water before the lights went off. They had been waiting for the farfalle and this time they weren't overcooked. They looked like perfect butterflies.

Judith saw the flickering lights in the distance. Most people seemed to have found candles. Maybe the others weren't home yet. When the children asked for refills she got up and gave them an apple each. There were nine left. "You don't need to brush your teeth tonight," she said. "And don't use the flush."

She took out a clean pot and turned on the faucet. When the water stopped she tried the bathroom, but the pot was only half full as she returned to the kitchen.

"I need to pee," her son said.

"Don't use the flush." Judith put her hand on her daughter's shoulder. "You watch him," she said and reached for a shopping bag. "I'll be back in ten minutes. You can both sleep in my bed tonight. It'll be very cold in here soon."

"Where are you going?"

"There's hardly any milk left."

Judith held up the candle stand. "Make a wish," she said and watched her kids thinking and then blowing. "Don't let anybody in," she said and went to the hall to put on her coat. She reached up to the top shelf and pulled out *The Woman in White*. She removed an envelope she'd stuck between page number 48 and 49 and shoved it into her bag.

Nine months before, a friend had told her that his wife kept making fun of him after he'd equipped the cellar with water cans and the mattress with cash.

"Everything would stop," he said after parking the car in front of her apartment house.

"What about phones?"

"Won't work. No app to help you out."

"We can still use regular ones, can't we? Most people still have them."

"Who would you call?"

"The police."

"What if they don't answer?"

She gazed up at the windows on the second floor behind which her children were sleeping. "The fire department?"

"They'd ask you if you had an emergency and if you didn't, they'd tell you to get off the line."

She reached for the door handle, saying, "Thank God our stove works with gas."

"Which is pumped up with electricity. Same with your water supply. The higher you live, the less you get. You can flush once, if you're lucky. And maybe fill a small bucket with tap water." He turned on the motor. "The first to go will be the old ones who don't get their medication. And the babies. Two weeks and you'll have us back in the caves, killing each other for a piece of bread."

When she was waiting that night for her feet to get warm under the blanket, she remembered a friend from Ireland who couldn't start a harvester one morning because the bank hadn't received the last payment and turned off the motor via satellite. She sent a text message to her friend and he answered that this was forbidden in Germany. She put her cell back, feeling relieved although she didn't even own a car. The next day, she'd gone to a hardware store to buy a 50 litre water can and on her way home she'd withdrawn a grand in small bills.

People on the sidewalk were talking and gesticulating to each other. Cars were moving slowly and traffic lights weren't working. Judith tried the grocery store door but it was locked. A man showed up next to her.

"Smartphones don't work," he said.

"No, they don't."

She crossed the street and walked to the next grocery

35

store that was bigger and open until midnight. People were standing in endless lines, trying to pay for their food but the scanners didn't work. They mostly took it calmly, except for a woman who held on to a packet of Pampers and ran toward the door.

Judith hid under a fruit stand until they turned off the emergency lights. Then she felt her way through the aisles and filled her bag with whole grain crispbread and zwieback. She was caught by a young assistant carrying a torch.

"You have to leave," he said.

"My kids are hungry."

"I'm sorry," he said.

They approached the exit.

A security guard aimed his torch at them. "You've got to leave that here, madam."

Judith opened her purse and took out a bill. "Please," she whispered. "I have two kids at home."

"Can't do that, madam."

"She's a friend. I'll pay for it tomorrow," the young assistant said.

Her son was fast asleep, her daughter still reading. "My phone's not working," she said.

"No smart phone's working. We can use the other." Judith blew out the candle. When she'd met the children's father, an ordinary candle lasted until next evening. They both took it for a sign, but he left them when the kids were six and two. He lived in Leipzig now with another wife and another kid.

Judith kissed her daughter on the forehead. "Go to sleep now."

"It's never been this dark, mom."

"Remember when we went to the countryside?"

"But there was the moon. And the stars."

Judith opened the curtain. "Have a look."

They stood next to each other until her daughter finished listing the names of the many stars her father had taught her, then Judith brought the shopping bag to the kitchen and unpacked it. Food wasn't a problem, it would last three to four weeks. She had read somewhere that people could live without food for another week or two.

She called the police and was told to stay calm. She called the fire department and was told to get off the line if there wasn't an emergency. For a split second, she thought of telling them that there was one but then put down the receiver.

"On the second day," her friend had said, "They will start looting the shops. And then you'll see. They'll become animals."

She crawled between the children and felt their warm soft bodies, listening to their regular breathing. Despite the drawn curtains, she could see everything. How quickly we adapt, she thought before falling asleep.

The next morning she called school and work and listened to the dial tone for a while and then put down the receiver. When the children woke, she brought them their winter boots and woollen caps and told them to wear a sweater and a cardigan. "It's kind of fun, isn't it?" she said.

"Yeah," her daughter said. "We would have had a written a test today."

Judith kissed her son's icy nose. "Let's see what we've got for breakfast."

"What about soccer? I need to go." He looked at the clock and said, "I'll be late."

"There's no school today," Judith said. "Everybody is staying home."

A friend of hers had once shown up with a box of ready-to-drink café latte; Judith found it too sweet and too artificial, but she hated throwing away food and thus left it in the cabinet for potential visitors who consumed such things. There were six cans. She would drink half a day. Maybe lengthen it with water. Eventually, she would appreciate anything that only smelled of coffee.

Her daughter opened the dishwasher to put away her bowl, but Judith reminded her that it wasn't working and so her daughter reached for the sponge and turned on the faucet. A few drops came out.

"Leave it there," Judith said.

"How do we brush our teeth?"

Judith took a cup and dipped it into the pot and passed it to her daughter.

"That's all?"

"Yep." She sat down again and watched her son eat. "Is it good?"

He nodded. There was a tiny piece of chocolate in the corner of his mouth.

"How about going for a walk?" She smiled at him. "Would you like that?"

"It's cold."

"We'll dress you up like Eskimos, all right?" She reached for his empty bowl and put it in the sink. Then, she heard the flush. She walked slowly out of the kitchen and came to a halt in front of the bathroom. "Honey, you have to listen to me."

Her daughter unlocked the door. "What?"

"I told you not to flush," Judith said.

"I'm sorry."

Judith looked her in the eye. "Promise that you will do exactly what I tell you in the future."

Her daughter frowned. "Calm down, Mom."

The street was full of people when they came out of the house. Some talked and some watched and some went back inside. A group of people was softly discussing something until a man came running. "It's only in Berlin," he shouted. "I just had my mother on the landline."

"The whole of Berlin?" a woman said.

"Plus Potsdam."

"Let's call Dad," Judith's daughter said.

"When we get home."

In front of a café people were sitting on benches, their thick gloves clutched around beer bottles. They were wrapped up in blankets and a cloud of smoke hung above them. Cars drifted along the street, unusually careful, considerate, although there were no policemen to replace the inoperative traffic lights. They walked past the closed shops and it felt like a Sunday. Then they headed home again and left their scarves and caps on during lunch (sandwiches). In the afternoon they played board games, sitting cross-legged on the carpet, held warm by blankets. At six o'clock Judith lit the second candle and prepared a meal of leftovers. She divided the rest of the orange juice between her children and wiped their dishes clean with toilet paper when they were finished.

She took the candle stand and led them to the bathroom to make them brush their teeth. "Put the lid down after you use the toilet."

"I have to go now," her son said and she waited in front of the bathroom until he was done and covered his turds with cleaner.

When both kids were sleeping, huddled against each other, Judith blew out the candle and fetched a can of latte from the kitchen. She left the apartment, walked down the stairs and opened a window. In the opposite building, somebody had the same idea; she could see an orange dot every now and then. She smoked looking at the star-covered sky. There couldn't be many cars on the streets; maybe people instinctively decided to save. Or maybe they really were at home now, in their bedrooms, producing the masses of babies everybody associated with blackouts.

Police cars of all types and sizes drove by the next day and informed via megaphones to not use vehicles. Despite the early hour, the street was full of people shouting and waving fists. Judith unpacked the battery-driven speakers she'd gotten for her daughter's birthday and connected them to her iPod. Townes Van Zandt was singing of mountains and rivers and valleys as she cut open the carton to get out the last drops of milk for the muesli. Her daughter sat down and yawned. She was wearing the thick woollen sweater that Judith had knitted for her two years ago before it vanished in the depths of the dresser having never been worn.

"Looks nice and warm," Judith said.

"Have you called Dad? Tell him to get us out of here."

"I'll do it later."

Her son looked suspiciously at his bowl. With the milk gone, she'd added water, but after another spoonful, he didn't seem to notice anymore.

"We have enough to eat and we have enough to drink," Judith said. "We just stay inside until it's over."

"And what are we supposed to do the whole fucking day?" her daughter said.

"Homework."

"I don't have any homework."

"Eat."

Her daughter looked at her, then she jumped up from the chair and ran into the hall. She'd already taken the phone off the hook when Judith arrived. She pressed it to her ear before finally passing it to Judith – there was no dial tone.

They studied in her son's room that led to the backyard. She turned off the iPod to save batteries. Her son was doing maths and her daughter wrote an essay about ten things she would take to a deserted island. After an hour they switched. When Judith wanted to help her daughter, she realized that she wasn't able to do the most basic calculations anymore.

For lunch, there was the last portion of pasta and afterwards, they shared an apple and yoghurt. She took out Monopoly from the children's large pile of board games. At six o'clock she went to the kitchen for zwieback and by nine o'clock she was bankrupt. Her daughter jumped up and let all her bills rain down on them.

They skipped brushing their teeth and Judith kissed them good-night.

"What if Dad doesn't even know?" her daughter mumbled.

When they were both asleep in her bed, Judith got up and peeped through the living-room curtains: nobody was outside. Maybe her friend had been wrong. Maybe most people would just stay indoors and wait for the lights to turn on again.

She went to the kitchen to get an empty plastic bottle. Then she put on her boots and coat, opened the door and listened. When she was sure that she was alone, she went quietly down the stairs. She unlocked the door to the cellar, filled the bottle with water from the can and hurried back up. Latte and cigarettes in hand, she walked down the stairs again, opened the window and smoked, counting the remaining cigarettes, trying to remember if she had one or two new packs in her drawer. The door next to hers opened and a dark silhouette came down the stairs.

"I'll give you a euro for a cigarette," her neighbour said.

"No," she said.

"Five."

"You don't have to give me money." She took out her pack and passed it to him. The tiny flame lit up their faces and they smiled at each other.

"Thanks."

"Sure," she said.

When they finished smoking, they went up the stairs together and separated in front of their doors.

The next day, when her children were sitting at the desk, working on the list of assignments that Judith had prepared for them, she locked the door twice and walked down the deserted stairs. She had the feeling that everybody except her family had left the building. She walked along the empty street, then turned the corner. There was a crowd in front of the grocery store; its windows were smashed. A man with a roll of toilet paper told her that there was no use going in anymore. She walked on and passed a kiosk whose owner was selling goods to the highest bidder. A bottle of water was just being exchanged for fifty euros.

There were no children. No elderly, no one showing any sign of infirmity, at least for now. Judith walked to the big grocery store. She arrived to see people attacking the security guards. More people came running out and within seconds the street was bursting with crowds who recklessly pushed their way through the smashed windows. Judith slowly retreated, happy that she wasn't carrying a bag; the ones who came out of the supermarket with their pickings were robbed instantly.

At home, the children had just finished their assignments. She made the last round of sandwiches with the remaining bread and the hardened chunk of cheddar. They sat down and ate in silence while Judith looked at them, feeling calm and safe in a way she'd never before. When they were finished, she opened the last yoghurt. Each had a spoon and passed it on. The children cleared the table while Judith fetched the Scrabble board. After using up the pieces, they invented stories with the words they'd placed on the board and then it was time for dinner again. They each had crispbread with butter and a glass of water. Then they lay down and Judith read them one of the books she'd saved from her childhood. It was about a girl who had to leave the village where she had grown up because her parents wanted her to go to school. Judith remembered her yearning to live in the country when the children were little, but their father only took it for a temporary fancy, and after he'd left them she couldn't summon the necessary strength for such a move.

She kept turning the tattered pages long after the children had fallen asleep. She put on her shoes and her coat and grabbed the half can of latte she'd saved from the previous day and her cigarettes. She opened the door, tiptoed down the stairs and opened the window. On the third drag, her neighbour came. She offered him a cigarette. They stood next to each other smoking and sharing the latte. When the cigarettes and the drink were finished they continued to look into the night and their hands joined.

The next day Judith organized a story contest. Her son was the winner. He'd written a story about a man who had lost his memory and woke up in a small village where nobody spoke his language. After lunch (zwieback with butter and an apple) they dressed up and pretended that they were a noble family on the Titanic and when it sank, they climbed into the lifeboat (the bathtub) and eventually reached a deserted island where they built a hut out of all the chairs they had. They covered it with clothes and bed linens and had a candle-lit dinner with crispbread and the last banana. Then, Judith searched the bookshelves for her songbook and they sang songs. When the children were sleeping, she grabbed a new can of latte and her cigarettes and went down

43

the stairs still wearing her evening dress. The neighbour was already waiting. After they'd tossed their cigarette butts into the night, their faces came close to one another and they listened to their breathing with closed eyes.

The next morning Judith remembered William Tell. She carefully opened the gilt-edged book and after a short quarrel about who would be playing William, they all studied their roles. They rehearsed the whole day and performed in front of stuffed animals. It was a big success.

"Why do we never open the curtains?" her son asked when Judith took them to bed.

"Because they keep out the cold," she said. "Remember how we had them like this for weeks last summer? And you were always happy to get here because it was nice and cool?"

"I wish it were summer now," her daughter said.

Judith laughed. "But we would have nothing to look forward to."

Later, when she wanted to wash herself in the bathroom, she heard someone moving in the hall. Still holding the wet cloth, she stormed into the dark and shrieked when she bumped into her daughter who was fully dressed. "What are you doing?"

"I want to see if Luna is okay."

"Are you crazy?"

"It's only two blocks, Mum!"

Judith pulled the key out of the lock. "It's dangerous outside. Don't do that again."

"And what about you? What are you doing out there? Plus, you're wasting water."

Judith got her dressing gown from the bathroom and when she came back into the hall, her daughter had already pulled off the boots.

"Why isn't Dad coming?"

"I don't know."

She waited for her daughter to undress and lay next to her until she seemed to be fast asleep. Then she grabbed the second to last can of latte and a blanket and slipped out of the apartment. After making sure that she'd locked the door twice, she sat on the stairs and lit a cigarette and another cigarette and another cigarette. When the latte was finished, she wrapped herself into the blanket and fell asleep. She woke up feeling her neighbour's embrace and they kissed and their hands wandered over their bodies until her daughter called, "Mum, where are you?"

Judith ran upstairs. Her son had wet the bed. "I'm here," she said. "It's all right."

Her daughter ran to the living room and flung open the curtains. "And what about this?"

A large group of people dressed in black, faces covered, armed with bats, hammers, and broomsticks were smashing the windows on the ground floors. Some had brought ladders. "We're too high," Judith said.

"What about the police? Why aren't they doing anything?"

"They'll be here in a minute, don't worry."

She pulled the children to the bathroom and undressed them. She fetched the water bottle from the kitchen and washed them. When they were wrapped up in towels, she took the rest of the water and washed herself.

"Now we'll die of thirst," her son said.

"Go back to sleep," Judith said. "We will not die. I'll take care of you. I promise."

When they'd fallen asleep, she went back to the living room and peeped through the curtain. It was quiet now. The people in black had disappeared. In their place stood soldiers with machine guns. Huge signs had been installed

45

forbidding people from leaving their homes. Thank God, Judith thought.

Dawn was breaking when she tiptoed down the stairs and into the cellar. She filled two bottles, hid them under her coat, and ran into her neighbour's girlfriend.

"You have children. You must have water somewhere," she said.

Judith hesitated.

The woman blocked her way. "I know what you're up to."

Judith shoved one bottle into her hand and ran upstairs. Back in her apartment, she pushed the furniture to the windows facing the street. She piled up dressers and desks and chairs, covering them with clothes and bed linens and when she was done they looked like mountains. In the bedroom, the children's faces were golden from the sun and she sat down on the floor next to them, looking at the bright blue sky. As the voices and the shooting grew louder she turned on her iPod and the children woke up to "Chelsea Morning."

"Tell me that I was only dreaming," her daughter said.

"This can't go on forever," Judith said. "Maybe it's harder than before to fix it but in the end, they will."

"It's been how many days? Five, six?" Her daughter closed her eyes again. "I don't even know."

Judith kissed her forehead.

"Three, honey. When we don't feel good it seems as though it has been ages, but actually, it hasn't been that long."

Her son climbed onto her lap. "Maybe everybody is dead by now and we're the only survivors."

"Nobody's dead, sweetheart." She put him down and stood up. "Listen, you both get fifty euros a day. Until they turn everything on again."

46

Her daughter sat up. "From the day it started?"

"From the day it started."

"Yeah," her son shouted.

"I'm older. I want a hundred." Her daughter grabbed her arm. "And what if they turn it on in the evening, will we still get paid?"

Judith opened *The Woman in White* again and took out the second envelope. She counted the bills into her children's hands. "You're getting seventy," she said to her daughter. "And I'll pay you every morning at nine o'clock unless the switch is working."

They were allowed to have breakfast in bed, zwieback and fresh orange juice made from the last orange, and she read them another of her favourite childhood books. It was about a young boy who was sold to a travelling artist. Judith proposed they act out some of the scenes. Her son wanted to be the monkey, so Rémi had to be played by her daughter. They travelled from village to village and performed their shows at the foot of the mountains and when night approached they asked the villagers for a piece of bread and a corner in their barn where they could spread out their blankets. They took their modest meal (half a zwieback each and water) at the campfire (three tea lights) and when the children were fast asleep, Judith put on her most beautiful dress, pinned up her hair, and carefully applied mascara and lipstick.

She opened her door. A trace of tea lights led upstairs. On the top floor, in front of the door to the attic that had been locked since they'd moved in, her neighbour had put up a tent. She crawled inside. Caressing him she could feel every bone. He pressed his face against her breast, she took him into her arms and they clung to each other like twin embryos in their mother's womb.

Back in her apartment, Judith divided all their provisions

47

in half, went down to the cellar and filled three bottles with water. She packed everything into a box, pushed it in front of her neighbour's door, knocked and hurried back inside.

In the evening her son had a fever. He looked so pale and lifeless that she became frightened for the first time. "He'll be fine," she said to her daughter.

"I'm bleeding."

Judith looked up. "What?"

"I think it's my period."

"We'll celebrate when this is over, okay?"

"What the fuck is there to celebrate? I want to go to Dad."

"It can't last forever, sweetheart. We'll all be fine."

Her daughter pressed her hands to her ears and shouted, "I want my dad!"

Judith went to the bathroom to get the thermometer and automatically reached for the light switch and it worked.

Visitors

They were from Kassel. They'd stayed to help cleaning up the mess after the party. They'd taken the empty beer bottles back to the store. They'd wiped the floor where somebody had puked. I'd thought that they were friends of my roommate's who'd left for Italy as soon as the DJ had packed up.

The only interesting thing about Kassel is *Documenta*, in case you don't know.

"It's just for a few nights," Oliver said.

"Mi casa, su casa," I said.

He, Frank, and Sabine took over the shopping and so there was breakfast, lunch, and dinner for a change. In return I ignored the racket coming out of my roommate's bedroom. Oliver said that he'd been dating Sabine, too, but it hadn't been like this then.

I smiled. "Are you two competing?"

He took off his glasses and started cleaning them with a corner of his shirt. "Aren't we all?"

Mostly, we were sitting in the kitchen and I was listening to their stories. On the first evening, they were talking about Raymond Carver and Gordon Lish. I remember the names because Oliver wrote them down for me. "It's a question of improving," Sabine said. She always had to move. Every other minute, she put a leg here or an arm there, got up, danced across the hall, came back to the kitchen, sat down, jumped up again. She wouldn't be easy to live with.

Scratching his back, Frank said, "What if you feel like it's not yours anymore?"

"He's dead," Sabine said. "Both are dead. So who cares?"

"There's a page on the internet," Oliver told me. "You

can see what Lish cut out. In the end, there was hardly anything left," he said.

I looked at the two boxes of Vermentino that Frank had bought at the Deli across the street. We were just finishing the sixth bottle. "There's no point in writing so much if people want only half of it," Frank said.

We cleaned up and sat down at the table again to go on with our drinking and smoking. Sabine said, "I wouldn't mind living here."

Frank put his hand on her thigh and thus kept her from jumping up again to do her dancing across the hall. He smiled at me and said, "I love your place."

He wasn't the first one to say so. But nobody knew how quiet it got when the parties were over. Fellowships were taking my roommate all over the world, and if he was home for a while, he left early in the morning and came back at night.

"It's so big," Sabine said.

In the beginning, we were five, and then one after the other moved out. My roommate got the place right after the Wall came down. Rent was two hundred marks then. They increased it a couple of times, but not enough to make him seriously look for extra roommates.

Sabine lit another cigarette. She'd brought a carton of *Fortunas*, out of which she'd just taken the last pack. She smiled and said, "Are you looking for a roommate?"

"Yeah," Frank said, "let's move in."

Oliver laughed. "Don't listen to them, Tina."

I reached for his tobacco and the papers. "Why not?"

When Frank and Sabine had gone to bed, Oliver read one of Carver's stories to me. It was about a blind man who came to visit and somehow the guy who told the story didn't like that, but in the end he drew a church or a cathedral, and the blind man held his hand.

50

Oliver took a piece of bread and went to the stove to dip it into the soup. "Awesome, isn't it?"

I said, "Yes."

"Look." He held up his arm. "Goose bumps."

I got used to them pretty soon. To their cooking and to their talking about things I knew nothing about. For example, while Frank was frying onions, Sabine once said, "I hate ballet moms," and he said, "Ballet dads are worse."

"No way," she said. "Moms love it, the pink stuff and the tiaras and all. Dads at least pretend not to care." Did I mention that she was running around in this sheer, short dress all the time? "They are waiting in a corner, reading their newspapers," she went on. "The mothers hang around together and keep chatting about how gifted their kids are. And they always have their crying toddlers with them."

Oliver said, "I thought we had an agreement." He started to roll a reefer. "We don't want to bore the hell out of Tina, right?"

Some of my friends had been running around with big bellies for a while and after that, they showed up with their babies. Then, they never called again. "I hold on to my cup of coffee," I said.

He smiled at me. "Sometimes life is merely a matter of coffee and whatever intimacy a cup of coffee affords."

Sabine said, "Got a boyfriend?"

"No," I said.

Frank filled a pita bread with the stuff he'd been frying in the pan and passed it to me. "Now you put salad on top," he said. It looked like the falafel at Hashim's kebab shop.

Sabine took a bite from her bread. The oil was running down her hands. "I'd love to have a place like that just for myself."

"What about parties?" Oliver passed her one of our

kitchen towels and said, "Aren't you inviting us?" He turned to me, put his hand on my underarm, smiled. "You wouldn't give a party without us, would you?"

I laughed. "If you clean up again, sure."

"You won't notice that we were here, promised," Frank said.

I opened the window, sat on the sill, looked down on the courtyard that for once wasn't quiet but echoed back our voices. "Before, there were friends hanging out all the time," I said. "They just came by. There was always somebody home."

"I know how it feels," Sabine said. "I never have the house to myself."

"All I'm asking for is a room," Frank said. "Last week, they killed my CD player with modelling clay."

"A room of one's own," Oliver said, raising his glass.

I wasn't as baked as not to figure out that they must have kids, but I was too baked to ask myself where those kids were right now.

"What about the agreement?" Sabine said.

Frank said, "Sorry, guys."

We had ice cream for dessert. Sabine drowned hers in whipped cream. "Remember *Quarkfein*?"

"Quarks are never found in isolation," Frank said.

Sabine laughed. "What is the matter?"

"Strange matter," Frank said, "very, very strange." He winked at me. "Isn't it, Tina?"

I smiled. "It is."

Oliver mixed another round of gin and tonics and said, "Any plans for tonight?"

Sabine got up and stretched herself, lifting her dress, showing her panties. She said, "I want to watch a movie at Hackesche Höfe. One of you guys wants to join?"

Frank didn't say anything, but he wouldn't let her go by

herself. Oliver looked at his naked feet. He was still wearing his PJ bottoms. He turned to me and said, "What about us?"

After Frank and Sabine had left, we went back to bed and watched Twin Peaks. I was a junior when they'd shown it on TV. My then boyfriend was really pissed because a week before the showdown somebody had written the name of Laura's murderer on the gym wall. At dusk we were done with the first season. Oliver said, "I also had a mattress on the floor when I began my studies."

I said, "And now a mahogany king size?"

"Why do you have the smallest room?"

I turned off the TV set. "To prevent myself from going to IKEA."

He laughed and put his glasses on the shoe box that served as my night stand. "If I moved, I'd need a truck."

"What's it like in Kassel?"

"There's *Documenta*." Oliver grinned and said, "You would get bored soon."

"I haven't been out of here for quite a while." I got rid of my t-shirt. I got rid of my bra. I said, "It's time to try something new."

He touched my neck and then slowly drove his hand downward, until it reached my belly button. "There's nothing new going on anywhere."

The others had just finished breakfast when we came into the kitchen. "It's our last day," Sabine said. "Let's do something nice."

"How about going to a lake?" Oliver said. "I'd love to take a swim."

I looked at him. I looked at his arms that had been holding me only minutes ago, at his warm hand that I'd felt on my skin.

53

Frank waved with his car key. "Get ready, sleepyheads."

I sat down at the table, waiting for the water to boil. Flipping through an old newspaper, I said, "So you're leaving tomorrow?"

Oliver put his arms around me and kissed my hair. "Can I borrow a towel?"

Sabine was driving. Frank sat next to her, holding her hand. Oliver read to me. It was Carver again, this time a story about a couple who first didn't want a kid, then wanted one, but in the end, after it was born, they weren't happy either. I liked listening to Oliver because he read as if he himself were the writer. As if he himself knew exactly how it felt to have a wife and a kid and everything else.

We swam and drank beer and smoked pot. Every now and then, one of us walked over to the snack bar to buy French fries or ice cream, but most of the time we lay in the sun and Oliver lay next to me. When it was getting dark, Sabine and Frank went for a last swim. Oliver was standing next to the water. He'd put on his jeans but was still bare-chested. "It gets fucking cold at night where I live."

I rolled up our towels, saying, "Rent is cheap in Kassel, isn't it?

He bent forward, grabbed a pebble, threw it into the water. "Not a clue," he said.

Sabine and Frank started packing as soon as we were home. Oliver went to my room and sat down on my bed. "Did I say thank you?"

I smiled. "It was fun."

"Give me a call when there's another party," he said. He rolled a reefer, and then he gave me the tobacco he'd just bought at the gas station. "I usually don't smoke," he said.

I started to comb my hair. It was still wet. "What do you usually do?"

Oliver slipped out of his chucks. Then he told me about their trip every year. He told me that Sabine was the only one who still lived in Kassel.

I said, "I don't get it."

"Sabine is married with two kids," he said. "Frank lives with his girlfriend. They have a daughter."

"And you meet only once a year?"

Oliver nodded.

I was waiting for him to go on with the family stuff, but he just said, "I feel so young again." He fell back and extended his arms. With the beard and his shorts, he looked like Jesus on the cross. Tomorrow night, I wouldn't have to share my mattress anymore. I said, "And what stories are you guys telling back home?"

Oliver lit the reefer and passed it on to me. "I don't know," he said. "I bet they are good ones."

"Well," I said.

He clapped his hands. When he opened them again, a moth fell onto my blanket, shook its wings, and hurried back to the corner where I'd piled up my clothes. "I live in Eckernförde," he said. "That's up north."

I stayed awake long after he'd gone to sleep because my back was burning. His arm was lying on my belly, and I didn't want to wake him by moving around. Listening to his soft breathing, I watched the green digits of my radio alarm clock. At dawn I hid his glasses behind the mattress, but before dropping off, I must have put them back again.

When I got up, they were gone. They'd cleaned the kitchen. They'd hung up the beach towels. They'd left a thank you note on the table.

In the evening, I sent an email to my roommate. I had a great time with his friends from Kassel, I wrote.

"What friends?" he wrote back the next day.

What You Want, What You Need, What You Get

He immediately recognizes her voice. It's me, she says, and he says, Hi, Lydia, and then she says, You have a son. Do you want to see him?

A son? he says.

Lydia suggests next Sunday. If that's okay with you.

He wants to ask her why she didn't get in touch before, but all he says is, Sunday's fine.

There's a photograph he took of her when they were on the Baltic coast; she is squinting against the sun, waving at him. He puts it against the pile of books on his night stand. She seems too young to become a mother.

The next morning he has breakfast at the café around the corner. A man holding a sleeping baby is sitting at the next table, reading a magazine. From time to time the man caresses its head. Then, suddenly, there is this woman with unkempt hair. She kisses the man on the mouth. They talk and they laugh, and, every other minute, they yawn as if they have just come home from a party. She takes the baby and puts it to her breast. It sucks and sucks and eventually looks to the side, exposing the nipple and a drop of milk running down the breast.

He tells his boss that he's got the flu. He buys his first pack of cigarettes after four years as a non-smoker. He drinks two bottles of Rioja a day. Her picture on the nightstand; he gently touches her belly, tries to visualize it growing.

One night they sat on a bench next to the TV tower. They shared a bottle of cheap wine and took off their clothes and jumped into the basins. They picked roses from the bushes and threw them into the night. At dawn he carried her back to the bench and she put her head on his lap and he carefully removed the petals from her wet hair.

After six days he gets up to take a shower and a shave. He arrives at the station much too early. Perhaps they won't come, he tells himself. He walks along the platform until the train approaches. She gets off, wearing a summer dress and high heels. He only remembers jeans and sneakers. And the leather jacket with the 'Enola Gay'-patch. Hello, she says, stretching out her hand that he barely dares to touch.

His son is tall. He looks like the guy from the student card he found on the bottom of the photo box. Except for the eyes, which are blue like the mid-morning Sardinian sea.

Lydia says, This is Finn.

Hello, his son says with a strikingly deep voice, hands buried in the pockets of his sweatpants.

I'll go for a walk, okay? She bites her lower lip. Seventeen years ago, she said, What do you want from me? and he said, What do you mean? and she bit her lower lip and he went to the kitchen to get another bottle of beer.

He clears his throat and looks at his son. You're hungry?

On the escalator he notices that his son's army bag is unzipped. You shouldn't do that, he says.

His son frowns.

There's a lot of pick pocketing around here. He stops in front of a *Burger King*. What about here?

I'm vegetarian.

They got fish.

His son raises the eyebrows. There's a scar above the right one.

He points at a bakery. A sandwich?

They leave the station with two cheese sandwiches. Have you been here before? he asks.

Sure, his son says.

Often?

Couple of times.

He sits down on a bench. His son moves away from him as far as possible, bending over his ludicrously large Nikes.

And, he says, do you like it?

His son removes the lettuce from the sandwich and throws it onto the lawn. It's all right.

Looking at his son's shoddy sweatpants, he says, You're still at school? He doesn't get more than a nod, but he goes on, And? He takes his son's shrugging for a sign that it could be better. Got plans for your future?

No.

He notices the long dirty fingernails of the right hand. The left hand hardly had any. Play the guitar?

Yeah.

Lydia sometimes joined him when he was practicing with his band. She sat next to the amp, reading a book. Once, he asked her to sing. She hesitated, then stood up, then took the microphone. Her voice was strange and beautiful. He looks at his son. He tries to picture Lydia singing him to sleep when he was little. You have a band?

No. His son stuffs the last part of his sandwich into his mouth, rummages his bag, produces a small metal box.

He imagines Lydia telling his son that his father played the guitar too. He imagines Lydia thinking of him when they went to a shop to buy the first guitar. I used to play, too.

His son nods, turning the box around in his hands.

He clears his throat and says, What kind of music do you like?

All kinds, his son says.

Come on, he says, which bands do you like?

His son takes a hand-rolled cigarette out of the box, lights it, takes a deep drag. The Stones, AC/DC.

He sniffs. You better put that out.

His son leans back, grinning. This is Berlin, right?

What about your mother?

She's fine with it, his son says. As long as I stick to the rule.

What rule?

His son takes a pair of sunglasses out of his bag and puts them on. Only weekends and holidays.

Then he often smoked pot. Lydia sometimes took one or two drags. Once, at a party in Kreuzberg, she smoked more than the usual and vanished after a while. Weeks later somebody told him that she had collapsed on the bathroom floor and that the paramedics had to be called. He looks around, wondering if she is watching. Your mother and I went to the gig at *Waldbühne*.

What gig?

Thunderstruck was the first song, he says, Fucking brilliant.

His son lets out the smoke through his nose, and says, O-kay.

He still has her mix tape. On the cover there is a collage of band photos, inside the titles in her neat handwriting. She must have spent hours with that tape and he only listened to it once or twice. When he wanted to listen to it last night, his tape deck wasn't working anymore.

A boy wearing a Bulls cap sits down on the next bench, dragging a girl onto his lap. She whispers something into his ear.

He says, winking, Your mum still looks great.

His son reaches into the pocket of his sweat pants, takes out a smart phone, starts writing.

Got a girlfriend?

Happiness is being single.

The speakers announce a regional train to Stralsund. That's where he took Lydia's picture. The condom ripped on the second night. She told him not to worry, so he didn't. I had no idea, he says, I would have taken care of you.

Eyes fixed on the display of his cell, his son says, No sweat.

He even helped her move. He helped her carry her stuff downstairs, drove the rented van to Hannover, helped her carry her stuff up to the top floor. He went to the balcony to smoke a cigarette and promised to visit soon. Then he drove the van back to Berlin. The two hundred mark deposit had been lying in his drawer for six months, before he finally managed to send it to her by registered mail.

His son finishes the water bottle and burps. Gotta go, he says.

He puts a hand on his son's shoulder. Give us a chance.

Why?

Cause you gotta know your father, he says. And I gotta know my son.

You can't always get what you want. His son lifts his sunglasses. That's what Carsten would say.

Who's Carsten?

Her boyfriend.

You forgot something.

His son's eyes. The colour of the Sardinian sea. His lips hardly opening when he says, Did I?

If you try sometime?

His son puts his sunglasses back on. Whatever.

Coming back to the station he realizes that Lydia has been watching them the whole time. She gets up from the bench and says, There you are.

There we are, he says.

To his surprise their son is able to smile. You're all right, Mom?

Lydia says, Did he behave? She checks her watch although there is a huge clock on the wall. Thank you for coming.

He smiles. What are your plans for tomorrow? He looks at their son, then at Lydia, then says, Can I invite you for dinner?

I'll call you, Lydia says.

She seemed so sure when she told him that she would continue her studies in Hannover. He didn't dare ask for the reason. He clears his throat, and then says, We could have rocked the thing together.

Lydia says, What do you mean?

Let's go, mum, his son says.

She extends her hand. He takes it, holds on to it, pulls her close. He puts his arms around her. Out of reflex probably, she embraces him. He feels her breathe out. He feels her relax.

And when his son tries to pull them apart, he turns around and takes him into his arms too.

Tell Me About France

When I wanted to close the door to my balcony, I saw my ex-husband stretched out on my new sun lounger. I hadn't heard from him in more than ten years. He'd lost weight and he looked exhausted, as if he'd been walking for a long time. And he was unusually pale for this time of the year. But I'd become immune to men not looking well. "How did you get up here?" I asked.

"Good to see you, Lin," he said.

Luckily, my daughter was already sleeping in her room. It had been hard to put her to bed then because she had this disease called Schönlein-Henoch, which took more than six weeks to heal.

"I'll be back in a sec," André said, and then he jumped over the railing. I looked after him and saw him running to his old Mercedes Benz, the one that took us to the South of France. He opened the passenger door and came back with a bottle of wine. "Catch," he said and threw it in my direction. I've had trouble seeing all my life, I'm very bad at catching things, but I held it in my hands a second later, laughing with relief. He grabbed the pole and pulled himself up. "Have you never tried?"

We met when I was sixteen. In my hometown I would climb over the balcony all the time, with my parents sleeping in the next room. I would make a loud ruckus in the bathroom, I would wash my face and put on my pyjamas and after saying good night, I would wait for half an hour, then dress and put on make-up again, in my room, with the help of a candle. André would be standing under the balcony, smoking and drinking beer, and I would jump over the railing to hurry back downtown with him. We broke up after graduation, but three years later met again and got married.

63

I went inside, for glasses and an ashtray. When I came back he was sitting on my lounger again. "Come here, Lin," he said.

I sank down next to him. "Where have you been?"

He raised his glass and carefully touched mine, as if he didn't want to make much noise, as if he knew that I had a little kid that needed sleep after being ill for so long. He smiled. "How are things?"

I shook my head.

"Tell me," he said.

I took a careful sip of the wine. I'd been drinking a lot after leaving my daughter's father but during her illness I hadn't had a drop, and I felt that I would soon be drunk. "What do you want?"

"Do you feel like going for a ride?" André looked up and said, "I just filled her up."

"The beast," I said.

"It's not the same one," he said. "Don't you want to give her a try?"

I thought of my daughter sleeping in her bed and shook my head.

André smiled at me. "When was the last time you were happy?"

I didn't answer. Happiness wasn't something I'd thought of lately.

"For me it was France," André said.

He'd been a student in Aix-en-Provence and I stayed with him as often as I could. It was my final year at school; I would have had much better grades if it weren't for him. The day the holidays began I would grab my backpack and hitchhike the 2000 kilometres south. The last time I went to visit him a truck driver picked me up near Valence and barely ten minutes later put his giant hand on my thigh but André's roommate had given me a gun. When I finally arrived in Aix, he said, "My grandfather would turn in his grave. This was designed to kill Germans, not to protect them."

André reached into the back pocket of his pants and took out a small bag of weed. He began to roll a reefer. I got up and said, "Are you hungry?"

He shook his head.

"Do you want to see the place?"

"I'm good," he said, putting the reefer onto the table, leaning back, closing his eyes. He suddenly looked very young again.

"You can stay the night," I said. "You can sleep on the couch."

"I'm good," he said again.

"I'll be back," I said.

My daughter was breathing regularly. There was a hint of a smile on her face. She was still pale and she had lost weight but I wasn't worried anymore. I bent down, inhaled the air that was coming out of her mouth; it smelled sweet again, like a child's breath. The blue marks on her arm had vanished, too. I was asked about them, and when I looked up I noticed the way they were looking at me, doctor and nurse, but then they found out about Schönlein-Henoch and their eyes became friendly again.

"I missed you," André said when I was back.

The lights of a plane circled downward. It would be one of the last to land tonight. A lot of people had demonstrated to ban night flights. Then they wanted to close the airport and there were demonstrations again.

"You don't know me," I said. "Not anymore."

He inhaled and held the reefer up to me. "Let me get to know you again."

"What if I don't smoke anymore?" I said. "What if I lived with somebody?" I took another sip of wine, thinking that this would be the last glass for me. "Would you have shown up like this?"

"I wanted to call you. You weren't in the phone book."

I reached for the reefer and took a drag. Weed always made me horny. I didn't like the idea of getting horny around my ex. I decided to only take a few drags. "Look," I said.

He looked at me.

It was the first time that I was sitting on my new balcony with somebody grown up. I often sat here on my own in the evening, reading a book until my daughter woke up crying. In the morning, with the air still clear and fresh and the sun on the other side of the house, I sat here with her on my lap, reading to her. But I never sat here with a friend before. "It's complicated," I said.

André put a hand on my knee. "Don't go away." He got up, jumped over the railing again, and was gone. His car is still there, I reminded myself, I would have heard him get inside and close the door and start the motor, I would have heard him driving away I sat leaning against the cool concrete wall for a while, but then I also got up and shouted into the dark. "André!"

He came out of the bushes zipping up his fly. "I'm here."

"I have a bathroom."

He went to his car to get another bottle of wine. He threw it to me again, and I caught it again, and then he climbed back onto my balcony and sat down next to me and our arms were touching. "Tell me about France," I said.

He reached into his shirt pocket and produced a pack of Luckies and held it up to me and I shook my head and he shrugged and took one out and lit it. "It was warm like now," he said. "We were sleeping on an airbed and in the morning, it was always flat. We didn't mind."

66

I'd just bought a mattress for eight hundred euros. I went to the store and they wanted to know where it hurt and I said, "Everywhere." I would still be paying for it two years later, long after we moved to a cheaper place, long after it had been stained with my daughter's pee and my menstrual blood.

"Once we drove to Avignon," André went on. "We forgot to get gas. The car stopped next to a rye field and we walked away from the road and made love."

"It wasn't rye."

He smiled. "I know."

"We didn't have money," I said. "We were starving." Every now and then I would wash my hair, which was very long and very blond then, and I would ask for an apple here and a piece of meat there and people would give it to me for free, while André was watching from a corner. "There was always Pastis," he said. "It made us forget hunger."

"That shit could have made us blind."

"We didn't care."

I reached for his cigarettes. "I quit," I said.

He held up the lighter. "I see."

I tried to ignore his body so close to mine. It was easier when we talked but I didn't know what to talk about and he didn't say anything. "Say something," I said.

He went with a hand under his T-shirt and scratched his back. "Do you want me to ask about your job?"

I shook my head. My GP had written me a sick notice for too long and afterward my daughter had been sick for too long, so I'd lost it.

"Let's do truth or lie," he said. "I begin." He gave me a push, gentle, but a push, and I jumped up. He shrank back. "Did I hurt you?"

"No," I said.

"I'm sorry, Lin."

I checked on my daughter again. I put my hand on her chest and my face next to hers and listened to her regular breathing and then I went back to André. "All right, let's play."

He lit another cigarette and had another sip from his glass, then he said, "My father was diagnosed with Alzheimer's last year. I'd just been asked to teach photography in Bern. I came back home a month ago to be with him while he would still remember me. He moved into an apartment with a view to the sea a couple of years ago." André finished and refilled his glass and then went on, "He still has his good moments, and when he does, we drive to the beach. Sometimes we play chess. I let him win."

"That's a lie," I said. "He can beat you in his sleep."

André grinned. "In the morning, a nurse comes over and I have some time to myself. I take a lot of walks. I missed the sea, you know? I didn't realize how much until I came back."

I liked his father. I liked both of his parents. After we got divorced I missed them more than I missed André. I continued to visit them for a while. They had a nice place downtown, in one of the very old alleys with the crooked houses that are more than five hundred years old. There are very narrow stairs leading up to the bedrooms; it must be hard to climb them in old age, with or without Alzheimer's.

"How old is he now?"

"He just turned seventy last month."

"What about your mother?"

"She died six years ago."

I looked at him, trying to see something in his face, anything that would have told me if I had been more watchful, but it was too dark. "Are we playing?"

"Of course we are."

"Let me get a candle," I said.

"Go ahead," he said.

"It's dark out here," I said.

"I'd like a candle." He smiled and said, "I'd like to see your face, too."

I went inside and got my new candle stand and placed it next to us on the ground. I lit the candles with André's lighter and said, "That's better."

"Your turn," he said.

I took a sip, thinking, This will really be my last glass. I took another sip and said, "Five years ago I fell in love with a med student. We moved together when he started working at a hospital. A year later our daughter was born. Her name's Jade. She was a couple of weeks old when it started. I don't think that he'd done it before, he himself seemed shocked and knelt down immediately to beg my pardon. He was always crying afterwards, pretending that he didn't know what he was doing. He even went so far as to offer seeing a psychiatrist. He told me about the meetings, but later I found out that he never went there. In the beginning it wasn't serious. Just a little blow. It was rather the thing to do it at all. In the beginning I could have hit back easily. Maybe he would have stopped then. But I wasn't able to. It was impossible to make a movement or even utter something. I just let it happen. Maybe that's what drove him to hit harder. At least he never did it in front of the baby. And then again, months went by and he was nice and polite and the perfect father. At work they seem to appreciate him and he got raises and better positions and everything. But then, all of a sudden, he would change again and become that monster. The last time he beat me unconscious when Jade was watching. I left the next day and went to a shelter. They helped me find the place here. I hated to leave town but they said it was better. It would be much more difficult to find us in Berlin, they said. But I'm still afraid. Hospitals work together, don't you think? He could run into a doctor from here and find out." I finished my glass and smiled and said, "Your turn again."

He started to roll another reefer. "When I was born I couldn't hear. Everybody thought that I was autistic, but then my mother went to a healer who told her that I didn't know the meaning of words. He made me listen to tapes of my mother reading a story but filtered to make it sound as if I were still in her belly. By and by, they took the filter out and in the end I was able to speak and understand language like everybody else."

I giggled. "That's a lie, right?" André had the perfect pitch. You could play him whatever song and he would be able to write down the notes. We often did that then. When we were listening to the radio and I liked a song I asked him to play it on the guitar and he just did it. I was very jealous. I practiced every day, and he just played whenever he felt like it, but he never worked on a song. He never worked on anything.

"It took a lot of trouble teaching me the right articles and verb forms. There is a time for developing a feeling for your native language and I was long past it. So I had a lot of training, but when I left elementary school, the whole thing was history."

"You don't remember anything?" I said. "The therapy and all?"

He shook his head. "A week before she died, my mom told me about it and gave me the cassette. She'd been hiding it because the healer said that I should never find out the origins of the strange noise. It was *The Little Prince*."

We bought the original version when we were in France and found it terribly silly. But it helped me improve my French, so we read it to each other.

"Do you still have your guitar?" André asked.

70

"No," I said.

He scratched his stubble, saying, "Isn't it strange that we stop doing what we once liked so much?"

I shrugged. "We all have to grow up."

"Meaning that we forget doing nice things?"

"Meaning that other things become more important."

"Like what?" He lit the reefer and took a drag. He took another drag, and then he passed it on to me.

I cleared my throat, and then I said, "Do you have kids?"

"Your turn," André said.

"I'm high." When we were getting high then, André and I, he became lazy and sleepy and I always felt terribly attractive and terribly in love. I tried to touch and kiss him, but he just leaned back and closed his eyes, and then he fell asleep and I sat there listening to music until loneliness knocked me out and I started to cry, knowing that it would be like that for the rest of my life.

He looked me in the eye. "Are you?"

I got up and reached for the watering can. I watered my flowers. I'd watered them before it got dark, but it was so hot and they wouldn't mind. When I moved in I bought pots and soil and seeds and after three weeks the first green sprouts broke through. Another three weeks and there were all kinds of flowers in all kinds of colours and it all seemed like a miracle to me.

"It's nice to see you doing that," André said.

I gazed down on the quiet street that still felt unreal and foreign. In the distance there was the hospital tower where they'd treated my daughter. One night I was standing behind one of the windows over there, trying to find our new place in the dark. I'd left the lights on just because of it.

"You were always able to turn the darkest den into a

home, no matter where we went." He opened his pack and took out the last cigarette. "A piece of cloth, a candle, some wild flowers was all you needed."

"When I was a little girl," I said, "my parents had friends in Kiel. Their son was my age. We played and ate crackers until we were put to bed next to each other. One night, we lay in his bed again and we were holding hands and then he said that he felt funny in his stomach and I asked him if it was because of the crackers and he said that he didn't think so and then I felt it in my stomach too. And we were looking at the ceiling, to which his parents had stuck stars that shone in the dark. When my father came into the room to pick me up, we pretended to be asleep, and he held on to my hand and I held on to his hand. After that I never saw him again because they moved to Munich." I put the watering can down and joined André on the lounger. "Your turn."

He put his arm around me and said, "After we got divorced I stayed in Italy for a while. I learned Italian at the American University of Rome and fell in love with a woman from California, who wanted to go home after the semester, so I went with her. She had a house near some huge dunes, and she had horses. When we split up, I lived in L.A. for a while and wrote a script that was turned into an independent movie. It wasn't a big success, but a man who had been diagnosed with cancer watched it and asked me to help turn his life into a film. He gave me a lot of money and all the freedom I needed and it is terribly experimental, but it was great fun to do it."

I tried to picture him as a father, leaning over a woman who looked like Zooey Deschanel. I'd just seen her in a movie. Americans like to have caesareans and epidurals, I heard, so perhaps they all look gorgeous after giving birth. "Did he really die?" I asked.

He chuckled. "What's your guess?"

We finished the wine. When the cars were back on the streets and the birds started singing again, we both lay down. I closed my eyes and said that I wasn't tired, that I only wanted to close my eyes for a while, and he said okay, but it was my daughter who woke me up again. I felt her hand on my cheek. She often did that then. She put her hand on my cheek as if she needed to feel that it was me, as if the sight of me wasn't enough. "Why are you sleeping here?"

I looked around. There were the glasses and the empty bottles and the ashtray with our butts. And there was the guitar case André had brought back from the States. I remembered the Rolling Stones sticker, the tongue. We went to California when we had been married for two years and I flew back alone. We didn't fight – we never fought – but in the States I realized that it wouldn't work out with the two of us when he came back to the hotel carrying the guitar case. "Joni Mitchell also plays a Martin," he said. I was standing in the doorway, watching him as he tuned his new guitar.

"Whose is it?" my daughter asked now.

"A friend of mine gave it to me."

"Doesn't he need it anymore?"

I opened the case, held the guitar. Then my fingers remembered a chord and another chord, and I remembered how I'd said to André that you can't just go into a shop and buy a Martin, that you have to earn it, like fucking Joni Mitchell earned it.

In the evening, after I had read to my daughter and put her to sleep, I dialled the number of André's parents. I still knew it by heart. I let it ring twice, and then I hung up. A couple of weeks later I called again and hung up again. Once, while we were having dinner, I heard a noise. I hurried out but it was just a flower pot that had fallen on the floor.

Right after Christmas we moved to a cheaper place. It had no balcony.

All the Forms of the Radiant Frost

Say, you're listening to the news in the morning. They don't mention snowstorms, but they do tell you to put on chains if you want to drive outside the city. Berlin will be safe, the authorities say; this year they are prepared. Last year they weren't. They had to wait until the ides of March for the ice to melt and the mess beneath to come back: piles of fireworks – some of them burnt, some not – empty bottles of champagne, and all the other items they'd used to welcome 2011. This year, though, everybody was ready when it started snowing, falling softly in the beginning, still melting on the ground. This led Michael to believe that it would be safe even if they went a little further away, not too far, let's say thirty kilometres from the city centre. And it led him to wake up his wife Nina, who wanted to spend another Sunday in bed. She did get up because she didn't want to discuss it anymore, because a word of refusal would lead to discussions, and that was something she didn't want.

Say, they were in the middle of nowhere now, at least it felt like it, and it definitely looked like it, with the snow covering everything. Michael steered the car along Bundesstrasse 101 and then turned into a dirt road that led to a little fish restaurant by a lake. He wasn't really hungry, and had he given it a bit more thought he might have guessed that Nina wasn't keen on returning to a place where she really had been happy, so happy that she had felt the urge to say it at least twice while munching on a piece of apple pie that was covered with whipped cream, and when he had bent over to kiss her, the scent of cinnamon made him reach for her mouth instead of her cheek. But Nina didn't care where they were going as long as she didn't have to make a decision. She just nodded, the way that she'd nodded in the morning.

Now the car was stuck and Michael had just called ADAC. But he wasn't sure if they would be able to find them. It was Nina who proposed to go back to the main road and wait for them there. Michael didn't like the idea. He didn't like the idea either to let Nina do the digging and wiping to keep the car clear, so she walked through the snow without thinking much, and she reached the main road, and she stood there, rubbing her hands, when an old BMW came to a halt next to her. "Just the right weather to hitch-hike," the driver said, rolling down the window.

"I wasn't hitch-hiking."

He switched on the interior light. "Maybe I can be of help anyway."

Nina looked at the cluster of fir trees behind which Michael would be waiting for her return. "Our car broke down," she said.

He reached over to open the passenger door. "I'll take you to the next station."

In the back, a baby was sleeping in a safety seat. "I'd better wait for ADAC," she said.

"Right you are." The driver smiled at her. "That one's a killer." He scratched himself under his T-shirt. Kurt Cobain's sad face stared out at her. "You will freeze to death here, mademoiselle."

It stank of full nappies and incense. Nina leaned back. She would get out at the next gas station and ask someone to take care of Michael and the car. She looked at the road. There were no tire marks in the snow. Theirs would soon disappear, too.

"Too hot?" The driver had rolled up the sleeves. His arms were covered with small tattoos. "I like it the Polish way," he said.

She started to unbutton her coat. "Polish?"

He grinned. "As the expression goes."

"Never heard of it."

He removed his baseball cap, ran the fingers through his hair, and put the cap back on. "It means that you turn the heating up all way. Like they do in Poland, you know?"

She looked at her gloves. Thousands of ice crystals mirrored the green dashboard illumination. Thousands of ice crystals, and not one matching any of the others. "My father had the same car," she said.

"This beast has been on the road for thirty years," the driver said. "I can take you to Grossbeeren. They've got a station there." He lifted his right hand from the wheel to scratch his beard stubbles. "My name's Tim. And the rug rat's Carlos."

A tiny shoe was attached to the rear-view mirror. It was bouncing back and forth, back and forth. "Sobotka," she said.

"Welcome on board, Sobotka," the driver said. "That's Russian, right?"

"That's my family name." She turned around. The baby was still sleeping. She would get out of the car, and the baby would never know that they had met. She touched the striped romper and said, "Who knitted this?"

"Not a clue. My missus had already worn it herself." He fondled the baby's foot and said, "Got kids, too?"

She shook her head.

"He wasn't on our agenda," he said, turning the radio on. "But you get used to it."

Kinder Egg toys where glued to the dashboard. In a few months' time, the little fingers would try to reach them. They would pull and pull until one got loose, and then they would quickly stuff it into the little mouth.

The driver yawned. "And all of a sudden, the next one is on its way."

"You shouldn't take a baby for a drive with such weather," Nina said.

"My missus has to study for her exams."

"I would never have let you go."

Turning the volume up, the driver said, "Snow wasn't on our agenda either."

She noticed the skull ring on his right hand that was moving to the beat. Some reggae beat. Surely he smoked pot. She bent forward to check on his pupils.

"Like father, like son." The driver winked at her. "He likes it real loud."

Eyes half-closed, Nina gazed at the masses of snowflakes bouncing against the wind shield. The summer before last, they had been searching half of Brandenburg for a place to call home. Michael had wanted their kids to be raised in the countryside.

The driver looked at her. "You're all right?"

"Do you live around here?"

He nodded. "My missus inherited the house from her grandma. But next year we'll move back in town." He opened the glove compartment, reached for a package of chewing gum, and said, "No rockin' an' rollin' out here." His skull ring got caught in her woollen shawl; he drew back his hand; she reached for it and held on to it, staring at the small tattoos, small like *Kinder Egg* toys, as the driver slammed on the breaks and they slowly drifted onto the oncoming lane, where they lingered for a while, so that Nina had time to look back once more, hoping to catch a last glimpse of the other car, but it was too far away and, despite Michael's digging and wiping, buried under the snow by now, and when she turned her head again, they had reached the shoulder, which was buried under the snow too, and they glided down the hillside slowly, and the snow protected them like cotton wool, until they banged sideways against an oak tree.

The driver moaned.

Nina turned around. The baby had woken up. It looked at her with very big and very green eyes.

"I can't move," the driver said. "I can't move my legs. Oh my God."

She opened the passenger door, stepped out of the car. The fender on his side looked like crumpled paper. She walked to the other side and opened the back door and took the baby out of its seat, saying, "Hello, cutie pie." The corners of the little mouth went upwards. There it was, the toothless smile. She returned to the passenger's seat and said, "My father used to say that a BMW and winter never made a good match. It isn't made for snow."

The man said, "Why did you do that?"

She turned off the music, leaned back, listened to the perfect silence. "Now that's better. Babies like Mozart, didn't you know?" She put her face next to the baby's, inhaled deeply. "Last winter, I was pregnant too. I put on Mozart all the time." She smiled. "Not the requiem of course."

He closed his eyes. Beads of sweat covered his front, but he was shivering in his T-shirt. The heating wasn't running anymore, now that the motor was off. Nina touched his arm. "Aren't you cold?"

"Please," he said, "You gotta call emergency."

"I forgot to bring my cell phone."

"Mine must be somewhere on the backseat," he whispered.

"You should wear a coat in this weather, shouldn't you?" She returned her gaze to the baby and said, "What about you, sweetheart? Are you all right?" The baby laughed. She tickled its neck, held it up, kissed its cheek, making it laugh even more. "You're heavy, little man." She rolled up one sleeve of the romper. The arm was chubby indeed. The baby certainly wasn't breastfed. (Breastfed babies don't get chubby.)

The man opened his eyes, slowly turned his head, said, "Will they see us from the road?" and Nina said, "How much does he weigh?"

The baby started to whimper, its body all tense. "Are you hungry?" Nina picked up the bottle. "This isn't breast milk, is it?"

"Please," the man whispered, "you gotta help me here."

She felt the rhythmic sucking. When the bottle was empty, she took a purse out of her coat. "Would you like to see my son?" She drew a photograph out of the rearmost case. "I knitted the pullover myself."

"This isn't funny anymore." The man was breathing noisily. "It hurts so much."

"It does," Nina said, "but they won't stop telling you that it will get better." She reached for the diaper. Last year, she'd bought some half the size. "I could have had a caesarean, but I wanted it the usual way." She took off the romper. The baby started to laugh again, shaking its arms. "We called him Maximilian," she said, unbuttoning the bodysuit, "Maximilian Jerzy Sobotka. Michael's grandfather's name was Jerzy." She rolled up the wet diaper and threw it out the window. (Day Two at Weekend Prenatal Class: caring for your baby; bathing, diapering, clothing.) "Michael is my husband," she said.

The man groaned. He had lost his cap. (Make sure to cover the little head, even inside.)

"I took the footprint," Nina said, "and one of his little hand." She buttoned up the bodysuit. "He was my baby, after all." She reached for the red snow suit. She'd bought one too. She'd shown it to Michael and he'd started to laugh. He said that it would hardly fit a doll. "I held him in my arms. I held him telling myself that he was only sleeping. That he would finally open his eyes, and his little mouth would search for my breast." She looked at the driver and said, I had so much milk. I could have fed your baby too."

Suddenly there was music again. It got louder and louder. No woman no cry. The man slowly lifted his hand. "That's my missus."

Nina took the key out of the ignition and said, "His heart stopped beating. There was only a week left, but the little heart just stopped beating." She wrapped her coat around the baby and opened the passenger's door. "No worries," she said, "I'll take good care of him."

She walked back to the road. When she saw the approaching lights of a car, she sped up. The driver surely would take her to Berlin; he wouldn't want a mother and her baby waiting in the cold. The lights were just above her as she stepped over a dead birch trunk, lost her balance, and fell backwards.

She landed on her back. The lights slowly faded. There would be other cars, she was sure about that, the most important thing was that the baby was okay. And it was. She had fallen but she had hold on to the baby. She peeped under her coat and laughed. "Look at you," she said, "You didn't even wake up." She lay in the soft snow, and the baby was keeping her warm, and soon, very soon, they would both be covered like Michael's car, like the BMW, like the whole of Brandenburg, and she smiled and closed her eyes.

A sharp cry woke her up. She sat up, opened her coat, whispered, "What's the matter?" Eyes closed, the baby began to search her breast (remember that nursing is not just about food – it's also about warmth, reassurance, healing, love). Nina pulled up her sweater. When the tiny lips enclosed her nipple, she felt the milk coming in. The baby sucked but didn't get enough and went back to crying.

And Nina cried too.

Let's leave them now. She'll be fine, and the baby will be fine. Everyone is going to be fine. See? Nina got up. She's reaching for her cell phone. She's looking at the sky where the clouds had broken. "Please help," she says.

And the sky is looking back at her, whispering, "There, there."

After the Commodores

Angie was the only one in San Jose, who had neither car nor license. She used to page me in the late afternoon, and half an hour later I would ring the bell at Black Rose's one-story house on South Side and she would open the door, still wearing her night gown. "What's up?"

And I would smile, with my breathing on hold to get used to the smell of perfume, wonder trees, and her body. "Nothing."

Hardly reaching my shoulders she weighed at least a hundred and sixty. She had a double chin and the small eyes of a pig. Her hair damaged from uncountable perms and colouring needed half a bottle of spray to stay in shape. All men were crazy about Angie, but she went for blacks only. "I have a new job," she said. "Let's celebrate."

"Can I work there, too?" My car was a gas-guzzler. I was slowly running out of money and I still had five weeks to cover before flying home. There was always my credit card, and there was always Steve, but he had his plans about the both of us, and I had mine.

We drove to Cougars. A tall guy with a base cap asked me if I wanted to dance. I said that I never danced with strangers, but he knew that I talked to strangers if they paid for my beer. "Everybody knows you." He smiled and said, "You're the crazy European."

I told him that I felt like driving to the beach. His eyes were fixed on the dance floor where a couple was dancing to the Chi-Lites. "I love that song," the guy said.

"So?" I said.

He put his half-full bottle onto the table. "Let's get out of here."

I steered my car though the deserted town, heading west. There were high concrete walls on both sides of the winding road, marked with traces of car paint in all kinds of colours. Every now and then, we passed a dried-up wreath that was hanging beneath a photo of a smiling man or woman. I pushed the start button of my tape player.

"Fuck Burdon," the guy said.

I turned up the volume and slammed on the gas. "It's your people he's playing with now," I said.

"Easy, woman," the guy said, putting his hand on my thigh.

"What's your name?"

He grinned. "Eric."

I parked next to the beach and asked him if he felt like taking a walk. He climbed onto the backseat. "All Germans want to come here and drive around in an old American car."

I looked at him through the rear-view mirror. I looked at his black skin on my ruby leather. "It's a pimp's car," Angie had said, when I'd picked her up the first time. "In the seventies, pimps drove such cars," she'd said. "Nobody would drive such a car today."

Eric said, "It's their once-in-a-lifetime thing."

I changed the tape and started to roll a reefer. Before I left Germany, I'd spent weeks mixing tapes. I didn't have a plan what to do, but I knew that I would buy a car, and that I would drive on highways, and that I would listen to these tapes.

Eric gently took the reefer out of my hand. "Having the moment of their life in the big fucking States of America." He inhaled deeply and returned the reefer. "Fucking a big black man on the backseat of their big American car."

"The grass here is a thrill," I said.

He stroked my neck, and then rested his chin on my shoulder. "What are you waiting for?"

He lit one of my cigarettes, rolled down the window, and checked on his face in the side mirror. I'd been meaning to ask why they only warned you of objects being closer than they appear on the passenger side but since I'd stopped sitting there I'd lost interest in that too. "Where do you live?" I asked.

"Just drive," he said and turned on the radio to some R'n'B station.

We shared my last chewing gum and headed back. He said, "turn right" and "turn left after the next intersection," and then, on King Road, in front of a prefab home, put his hand on my thigh again. "See ya."

I felt them there, sleeping in their beds. His big family who would have breakfast in a few hours. At a big table covered with all kinds of cereal, fluffy white sandwiches, a gigantic peanut butter jar, half a gallon of low fat milk. And him sitting on a chair in the corner, drinking coffee, yawning.

"See ya," I said.

Steve was washing down his vitamins with orange juice when I got back. I quickly walked by and locked myself in the bathroom.

He knocked at the door.

I looked at the mirror thinking that I was looking at a woman who had just fucked a big black American.

"Talk to me, please," Steve said.

I took a shower. When I came out of the bathroom, he had left.

Later, at one of the happy hour places on Market Street, I went to the bar to get two beers while Angie filled our plates at the buffet. "You gotta get out of that place," she said and put a huge bowl of Cesar salad onto the table.

"I don't have money."

She was nibbling at a chicken wing. Her fingers were greasy, shiny. She licked one after the other clean and then said, "We'll find you a job."

The men at the next table had been watching us. They paid for our second beer. Smiling, we raised the cold bottles. They joined us after a while, but they were white and Angie was in a hurry to leave.

In her room, there was a bed, a closet, and a sideboard full of cosmetics, hair products, and cheap perfumes. She threw a bunch of dresses and skirts onto her unmade bed. "You're cute, you know" she said, "but you gotta show it."

I reached for a black dress. "How about that?"

"Too sophisticated."

Her head slightly bent she was watching me slipping in and out of her clothes. Sometimes she made a knot here or pulled the fabric there but let go in the end. "Let's do some shopping," she said.

I watched her putting on fake nails. "I'm going back next month," I said. "It doesn't make sense."

She held her hands up, waiting for the cherry polish to dry. "Back where?"

We were about to leave when Black Rose knocked on the door. "Ladies," he said, lying down on Angie's bed. "What's up?

She crawled next to him. "Rita's looking for a place to stay."

He let her take a drag from his reefer. Her skin was even lighter than mine. Their legs next to each other looked like giant piano keys.

86

"The guy she's living with is a jerk," Angie said.

I sat down on the floor, leaned against the wall.

Black Rose bent over and passed me the reefer. "What's it like in good ole Germany?"

I was getting high. "Germany?" I said. "Where the fuck is Germany?"

"We gotta find someone to marry you," Angie said. "You suck dick a couple of times, and then you'll get a divorce."

"All right," I said.

She reached for her cigarettes. "We won't let you go, honey."

Black Rose looked at my legs. "You can have the room across the hall," he said. "We'll put some paint on and maybe get a new carpet. How does that sound?"

I knew that Angie didn't lock her door when she couldn't pay the rent. I returned the reefer, smiling. "When can I move in?"

We were sitting in the backyard next to the pool that hadn't been filled with water for a decade. Instead it housed broken fridges, washing machines, and heaps of garbage bags. It was eight o'clock in the morning, so the sun was still having mercy on us. We'd just come home.

Angie had swiped two Coronas from Black Rose's fridge. "He's mad at me anyway," she said, glancing at the windows behind which everybody was still sleeping. "He blames me for the last phone bill."

Two days ago, I had called my parents in Germany. They had told me that my boyfriend was planning to pick me up at the airport. I had told them a lot of things, but I hadn't told them that I was planning to stay. "What if he kicks you out?" I said.

"There are rooms all over town." She got rid of her tight

dress. I often felt too fat at the beach and sat there without taking my clothes off. Angie seemed comfortable everywhere, naked or not. "You're too serious," she said and lit one of her menthols.

"Am I?"

She blew rings into the air that was getting warmer every minute. "All Germans are too serious."

A friend of Angie's knew a guy selling green cards. We picked him up at KFC. He told me to park the car in Santa Clara, next to a villa that looked as if it had been flown over from the Mediterranean. "Wait here," he said.

I watched him crossing the street. He looked like a college guy who wanted to get the assign papers of a friend. "The airplane is leaving in ten minutes," I said to Angie.

"What airplane?"

"The one supposed to bring me home."

"You are home."

"What if he just told shit?"

She leaned back. "Objects in the mirror are closer than they appear."

I cut off Jim Morrison singing about strange people and said, "Can you be serious for once?"

She turned on the radio, searched for a station until the Commodores filled the car, sang, "*That's why I'm easy.*"

I turned down the volume. "I will be illegal. Actually, I'm illegal now."

"*Easy like Sunday morning,*" she sang, turning up the volume again.

The guy stepped out of the villa and gave us a sign. Entering the hall, I felt like in a movie. The cleaning lady must have left only minutes ago, it still smelled of Purex. We went to the second floor where a young kid with a military cap was waiting for us. He was wearing shoddy sweatpants and a shirt he probably hadn't changed in a week. "How's it going?" he said, extending his tiny hand.

I was taken aback by its cold. I wasn't used to cold things anymore, except for beer bottles. "All right," I said.

"You can call me Mahler," he said.

We followed him into his room. The curtains were drawn and the only light came from a floor lamp. "Like the composer?" I said.

"No," he said, "Like *Horst* Mahler." He looked at me and said, "So you want to be American?"

I cleared my throat. "Well."

Angie said, "You're dead right, kiddo." She let herself fall onto the mattress that was lying on the floor. I stayed put next to the window. Apart from a desk there was no other furniture. The kid and Angie's friend sat down on beer crates. We weren't allowed to smoke inside, but we were forced to gulp half a dozen of Tequila shots. I was drunk soon and sank down next to Angie, who was holding a cigarette without lighting it.

Fumbling with his cap, Mahler talked about Che Guevara and communism, and how he'd believed in the GDR where he once had a pen friend, and how disappointed he was when this pen friend moved to Munich for a better job after the revolution. Mahler liked to say the word revolution. He said *ree-volution,* pausing after the first syllable. Then he jumped up and said, "Got the picture?"

Angie searched my bag and took out the envelope that the man at Foto Express had given me in the morning. The picture was wrapped in my last savings. Black Rose wouldn't expect the rent before Friday next week, but I was getting ready to leave my door open for him.

Mahler stuffed the envelope into his cap and put it back on. "I'd do it for free, but you got to have principles."

As we were heading downtown again Angie's friend told us that Mahler's father was a fundamentalist republican, who saw himself as a crusader against illegal immigration. Angie's friend had told Mahler that my father had been a famous member of the SED.

"I grew up on the other side of the wall," I said.

The guy grinned. "Commies get it for half price."

Three days later I had my green card. Angie and I went to Cougars to celebrate. "Miss America," Angie said, "Got any plans?"

I ordered two beers. "The sky is the limit," I said.

I stayed at the bar to keep an eye on the entrance, but there was no sight of a big black American wearing a base cap. Angie was asked to dance. A couple of songs later she wanted to go to a party, but I said no.

She hugged me. "You're not mad at me if I go?"

"I'm not," I said.

"His friend is cute," she said. "You should come along." She stepped back to wave at somebody. The guys around us were staring at her tight velvet dress that would soon land on the floor of somebody's bedroom.

I kissed her on the mouth. "You have fun, honey."

My beer was nearly empty. I thought about ordering another one, when a white guy wearing a tank top said, "Can I get you something?" He took my empty bottle and showed it to the girl behind the bar. "I dig your style." I had skipped the fashion show today and put on my Levi's and an old, loose t-shirt. The man took out a pack of tobacco and started rolling a cigarette. "I dig your Cadillac too."

The waitress passed me another Beck's. I put my hand around the cold bottle. "Thank you. For the beer I mean."

"It's German, isn't it?" the man said.

"They make it in my hometown."

"I've never been to Germany. I'd sure like to visit."

When I'd boarded the plane three months before, it had been snowing. This guy, who looked like a surfer with his long, sun-bleached hair, most probably had never seen snow before. Never picked it up to form a ball and then throw it. Never tasted it. Never felt it melting on the skin. "It's fucking cold over there," I said.

He smiled. "It can get very cold here too. Better keep your coat on."

The Last Planet

He broke up with her after they'd finished desert, which was *crème brulée*. He said, "There is something I need to talk about."

"Tell me," Suzanne said, leaning back. She combed her hair with her fingers and started to braid it. She did that when she got ready to listen to somebody for longer.

Phil said, "I want to break up with you."

She let go of her hair, took a napkin, wiped her mouth, and said, "Why?"

A few tables away, a man his age was sitting with one of his former students. She had graduated in June. Phil smiled as she waved at him.

Suzanne leaned forward. "You're not sick, are you?" she said. "Do you want to spare me the truth?"

"I'm not," he said.

"I was once going out with somebody who committed suicide. He also split up with me three months before without telling me why."

He laughed. "I'm fine, don't worry."

She opened her mouth as if to say something, and then she closed it again.

"Excuse me," he said and got up.

While he was washing his hands in the bathroom, his former pupil's cavalier showed up, extended his hand and said, "Nice to finally meet you, Mr. Renner. We owe you."

The paper towel spender was empty. Phil dried his right hand on his jeans and let the other man grab it.

"She took her time, but in the end she got the message." The man patted Phil on his shoulder with his free hand and said, "It's always helpful to have a crush on the teacher. Gets the brain going." He grinned. "You gotta love if you wanna learn. I owe my graduation to Mrs. Kowalski. Poor woman died of breast cancer two years later."

"Well," Phil said. "I was happy to hear that Muriel did so well. She was top ten, wasn't she?"

"You bet!" The man's eyes got bleary. "It's not easy when they grow up. They are a pain in the ass, and then they become as sweet as sugar again, just before leaving you for good." He let go of Phil's hand and began to unbutton his fly. "That's how it goes."

"Have a nice evening," Phil said and reached for the door.

"You too." The man turned his head around, smiling. "That is exactly the kind of woman I would have a nice evening with," he said. "Your wife?"

"No," Phil said.

"Ask her," the man said. "She's waiting for it."

Suzanne and Phil finished their coffee and smoked a cigarette in front of the restaurant, and then he asked if he could take her to the bus, which she declined. He looked after her as she walked down the street, and when she had vanished around the corner, he smoked another cigarette and went home.

The first week he didn't notice the change. He took out his cell phone from time to time to call her and then realized that he had no reason to do so. One night he was having a nightmare and felt like telling her, because she had been having nightmares regularly and was wondering about him never even recalling what he'd dreamt. She liked to tell him her dreams. Usually, he was half asleep then.

At the end of November he was asked to sub for the history teacher. Phil taught English and French and had graciously failed in history at school. "Just the basics," his boss said. "Until we find a replacement."

93

When Phil called his colleague in the evening he told him that he'd been diagnosed with prostate cancer. "Sorry," Phil said, "Won't keep you up for long. Can you manage to have a look at the tests?" He cleared his throat and went on, "Thing is, I need a couple of history lessons myself first."

"Sure," his colleague said, "come around any time. We'll have a cup of coffee. Don't know, mate, people seem to think that I'm contagious."

Phil looked at the pile of books the head had given him. "Next week I'm rather busy," he said. "Would you mind if I send a messenger around?"

"No worries," his colleague said. "But come around another time, will you? I just got a new espresso maker, the taste is hilarious. How is school anyway? Couldn't wait for the holidays before and now I'm really missing it. Fuck," he said, "I'm frightened. I really am. But thanks anyway for taking over. And come by for a coffee, mate. I'd really appreciate it."

"I'll call you," Phil said and hung up.

He spent the weekend browsing the internet to update his knowledge on World War II. There were some names he remembered but usually in the wrong context. He got lost in Wikipedia and decided to call it off at five o'clock in the morning. When he lay in bed, he had to think of Suzanne. He told himself that he missed having sex with her. The next day he plunged back into his history crash course, taking meals at the desk, with the only interruption in the form of a phone call from his father, who told him how his mother was doing. Phil promised to visit soon.

"You might want to do this on one of the next weekends," his father said.

Browsing over the definition of *Appeasement*, Phil said, "I'll see what I can do."

"Of course," his father said. "How's school?"

Phil used it as an excuse to hang up and went back to work.

He was two stops away from school when the girl sitting next to him started to vomit. The bus driver left his seat and told them to get out. "Getting on a bus pissed like this," he said. It was useless to explain, so Phil led the girl out and made her sit on the bench at the bus stop. He rummaged in his bag for his cell to call the secretary and a taxi. "Don't worry," he said to the girl.

She was crying. With all that make-up she'd seemed grown-up at first, but now he realized that she couldn't be older than fifteen. She must have been partying. Like his son. His mother had called him a few weeks ago to say that she was worried; somebody had seen Leander on Alexanderplatz, with a bunch of other youths, passing around a vodka bottle. He told her that it wasn't serious. He told her that he would get over it. "I'll take you home," he said to the girl. "Where do you live?"

She was shivering.

"Give me your sweater." He took off his jacket and said, "You can wear this."

The girl turned to him, and then she raised her arms. She looked even younger now. Phil rolled up her sweater to keep the vomit inside and pulled the collar over her head. The girl bent forward. Like his son, when he had thrown up as a child, and they came running into his room, helping him out of bed, holding him, and when they were sure that there wouldn't be more, they would carefully remove his pyjamas, take him to the bathroom, put him into the bathtub and shower all the vomit off of his hair and his skin, and then Phil would carry him back to his room and Leander would fall asleep on his arms while Nathalie changed the sheets.

Phil hung his jacket around the girl's shoulders and said, "I can't do anything about your pants though." He marched toward the taxi, opened the back door and sat next to the girl on the backseat. "We have to tell him where to go."

"Wilmsstrase," she said and when they stopped in front of a four-story apartment house, he said, "You'll manage?" and she nodded and got out.

He told the driver the address of his school after he'd watched her take a key-ring out of her bag and open the heavy front door. Then he turned around once more: The girl sat crouched on the floor, her hand still on the door knob. He paid the driver and got out.

The walls in the hall were covered with photographs, a row of large ones in black and white surrounded by dozens of small colour snapshots. The girl reached for a photo that showed a smiling man with shoulder-long dark hair and a beard. She smashed it onto the floor, and then sank down and freed it from the splinters of glass.

He took her in his arms, saying, "Where's your room?"

She nodded toward a door with a wooden plate. The name MILENA was carved into it. He carried her to the unmade bed, stepping around the clothes scattered on the floor. She sank back, her father's photo pressed to her chest.

He sat on the carpet next to the bed. She fell asleep. He gently let go of her hand and covered her with the pink blanket that was lying on the floor. Then, he went back to the hall where he'd seen the phone and a pin board with postcards and more family pictures and numbers. He found "Mom" and was told to try again later. He rang "Dad" too, listened to the ring tone and then to a warm, friendly voice that promised to get back as soon as possible if he left his name and number.

He thought of them returning and finding him in their apartment, with their teenage daughter, and called Suzanne.

The girl was still sleeping when she arrived. He got up and answered the door, and then he led her into the girl's room. "Thank you. I really appreciate it."

"I'd be happy if someone took care of my kid in a situation like this," Suzanne said.

"I'd get a shock coming home, finding my daughter pissed, in the company of a man twice her age."

"Thrice." She took the crumpled photo out of the girl's hands. "Maybe he left them."

He shrugged.

"We should wash her." She touched her hair, and then she touched the collar. "She's all wet. We should take that off." She lifted the blanket and said, "What a mess."

"Her parents will be home soon," he said.

Suzanne went out of the room and returned with a bowl of hot water and a cloth. She removed the girl's shirt and pants and washed her. The girl groaned in her sleep. Suzanne whispered, "When I was young, I had a friend who lived next door. She liked to wash my hair and brush it. She would make braids or pin it up as if I were a bride. She had very short hair herself."

He looked at his cell to check on the time, went back to the hall and tried once more to reach the mother, but her cell was still switched off so he left another message for Dad. "Maybe she has a brother or a sister," he said as he sat down next to the girl again.

"I'll find out." When Suzanne came back, she said, "A brother. Around nine or ten, I'd say." She smiled. "He likes Lego."

He put his hand on the girl's forehead. "She's hot."

"It's good that she's sleeping," Suzanne said.

When Leander had been a baby, one of them stayed home while the other was attending classes at university. It was usually during Leander's nap that they met for half an hour to have a cup of coffee together and exchange the latest news: half of the students had failed in Middle English; the strike had been prolonged; Leander's bottom was sore.

Suzanne went to the shelf with the CDs and said, "She's listening to The Smiths. I was into The Smiths."

"Probably her parents' collection," he said.

"I had all the records." She opened a CD and sang softly, "Please, please, please, let me get what I want." She went to the dresser and sniffed at the girl's perfume bottles. "I had to share a room with my little sister. The only place where I could lock myself in was the bathroom."

The girl sighed in her sleep and turned around.

"I was dreaming of my brother the other night," he said. "I dreamed that I met him on the street." He paused and after a while went on, "We were both grownups."

"You never told me that you had a brother."

"I was a baby when he died."

Suzanne got up. "I better pick up the broken glass."

He leaned back. He listened to Suzanne's steps, and then he listened to her talking to somebody. She came back to the girl's room, followed by a boy. "My friend here brought your sister home," she whispered. "She was sick on the bus." She put her hands on the boy's shoulder and said, "Can you show me where you keep your tea? Your sister will like a hot tea when she wakes up."

Phil said, "Don't you have to be at school?"

"Our teacher took us to Natural Science Museum." The boy looked at him frowning. "Where's Mom?"

Suzanne said, "We tried to call her. Do you have any idea where she might be now?"

"She's working," the boy said.

"Do you have her number at work?"

The boy pointed at his sister. "She does."

When they were gone, Phil called at school. "I have an emergency here," he said. "These tests, have you sent them over already?" He listened, then said, "Never mind."

The girl opened her eyes.

Phil put his cell down and smiled. "I called your mother. She's not answering"

"She's with Dad."

He looked out the window. The branches of a huge tree were slightly moving. There were only a few leaves left, which hung down like sleeping bats. A nest with baby birds sat lonely and unprotected in the centre of the crown. They were stretching their heads up, beaks wide open, crying for their mother, hungrily, anxiously.

He turned to the girl again. "Your brother just got back. He's in the kitchen with my girlfriend."

The boy was sitting at the table that looked like a still life composed of four plates, four cups, four knives and leftovers from breakfast. Suzanne passed hot cocoa to the children, then turned to Phil and said, "What about you?"

"I'd die for a coffee," he said.

The boy looked up. "Suzie used to work at the Natural Science Museum."

Phil smiled at Suzanne. "You never told me."

"That was a long time ago." She turned back to the children and said, "Do you want me to cook something for you? You must be hungry."

"No," the girl said.

"I'm starving," the boy said.

Suzanne stroked his hair. "Just tell me what you'd like to eat."

"Pizza," the boy said, "Daddy promised to make pizza."

Phil reached for his own cell, saying, "Shall I order one?"

"We always make it ourselves." The girl put down her cup, stood up and walked over to the fridge to take out tomatoes, yellow peppers, mushrooms, and mozzarella. "Get the onions," she said to her brother. Then she turned to Phil. "Do you know how to make the dough?"

"It takes too long," he said. "Let's make something else."

"I want pizza," the boy said.

Suzanne reached for an unopened packet of organic flour and put it onto the table. "I want Pizza too."

"Right." Phil rolled up his sleeves. "We used to do it on the table." He went to the sink to get a cloth. "But I need some space first."

The boy took the dirty plates and cups to the sink. "Tell her about the museum," he said to Suzanne. "Tell her what you told me."

"Yes," Phil said, "Tell us all."

Suzanne crossed her arms on her chest and said, "When I was a student, I first got a job as a ticket vendor. They organized birthday parties there but once one of the assistants became sick and I had to replace him. It went well and so they offered me to do it regularly."

"Tell them what you had to do," the boy said.

"There was a huge circular screen attached to the ceiling and beneath it there was a round sofa. When the show began, the screen would slowly come down. You first saw the universe, and then everything was a big fireball until by and by our planet was born. I had to tell them what happened when and of course they had a lot of questions, so I had a remote control to stop the movie or rewind it." She smiled and said, "If they wanted to see a certain planet, I bought them closer."

"They took away Pluto," the boy said. "It was always there and now it's gone."

Suzanne looked at him and said, "It's too small to be among the big ones. If they'd kept Pluto, it would have been an invitation to at least forty others."

The girl put a bunch of basil next to the tomatoes. The whole kitchen suddenly smelled like an Italian restaurant. "Wouldn't that be great?" She cut the mozzarella into slices, ate one of them, then passed a slice to her brother. "Just imagine!"

Phil laughed. "Do you want to learn all of the names by heart?" He poured the flour onto the table and said, "Future students would hate you. It's difficult enough to memorize the ones that are already there."

"Do you know them?" Suzanne winked at Phil. "Do you?"

He spread the flour across the table and made eight holes. He took a glass, filled it with water, slowly dripped it into the first hole. "Mercury." Then he filled the second hole and said, "Venus."

"Let me do it," the boy said.

Phil passed him the glass. "Be careful."

"Don't help him with the names," Suzanne said.

"Earth." Phil smiled at her and said, "Mars, Jupiter, Saturn, Uranus, Neptune."

The boy made another hole and said, "And here's Pluto."

She must have been standing in the doorway for quite a while, watching them. Phil turned around. She stood there as if she too was waiting for something, someone to tell her what to say.

Suzanne cleared her throat and said, "We're making pizza."

The woman nodded. Then she said, "That's right. My husband promised." She waited until Phil and Suzanne had washed their hands and then walked them to the front door. "He had an accident." Looking past them, she breathed in, and then she breathed out again. "Milena ran away from the hospital." She cleared her throat and said, "Where did you find her?"

"On the bus," he said.

The woman looked at the space where the photo was missing. "Thank you."

Phil wrote his cell number on the note pad that was lying on the shelf. "Please call if I can be of any help."

The mother bit on her lower lip and nodded.

Suzanne grabbed his sleeve. "Let's go."

She had come by bike but offered to accompany him to the subway station. They walked the three minutes in silence and when they reached the entrance, she took out her pack of cigarettes. She held it up to him and then took one herself. "How did you know it was your brother? He was still small, wasn't he?"

He inhaled deeply, blew out the smoke, said, "I knew it was him."

Suzanne flipped away her cigarette and got on her bike. "Take care," she said.

He opened his mouth but above them the subway approached with brakes squealing so he closed it again. When it stopped and the noise stopped too, he couldn't see her anymore.

Stains

Three days after the summer holidays were over our father came home from work early, drove us downtown to the new ice-cream parlour, and told us that our mother had been taken to the hospital. We were allowed to have as many scoops as we wanted. My brother Milan threw up in the car when we were only a block away from home. Our father drove on and parked the car in front of our apartment house to let him out and I was sent to get Lysol and wipes. When I came back, my sister Andrea was sitting on the curb, counting her mosquito bites. Our father was leaning against the car. He said, "Where are your glasses?"

They were hidden under the pile of sweaters in my closet. "I lost them," I said, sinking down on the curb, too. I held up my leg and said, "Thirty-eight."

Our father started cleaning up the mess on the passenger seat. Milan came out of the house, grinning. He had changed and put on our father's new sunglasses. "Are you out of your mind?" I whispered but he just showed me the middle finger. Since he'd turned fifteen he was showing off. Within a couple of months he had become a head taller than me. Sometimes, I still tried to fight with him, just to touch his new muscles.

Our father closed the doors to the car and threw the dirty wipes into the trash, saying, "Do you want to sit here all night?"

"You're going to fall," I said, pointing at Milan's loose shoelaces.

He kicked me. "Get lost."

That night my sister crawled into my bed. We could hear soft music coming out of the living room. From time to time, I heard my brother and my father talking. Lately, they often sat in the living room before going to bed and our mother came into my room after singing my sister to sleep. Once, she asked me to put nail polish on her fingernails. She never wore nail polish. It looked strange on her hands, like blood. Or she would say things like, "I'd like to be thirteen again." "Would you really?" I asked. And she shook her head, laughing. "Of course not. But it's nice to see my girl growing up."

Now, Andrea sat up and said, "When is Mommy coming home?"

"You heard what Dad said." I yawned and turned to the wall. "Go to sleep."

"He said after the operation," she whispered.

"See?"

"But how long does it take?"

I reached for her hand, held it tight. "Remember what they said in the book when the tiger had the operation?"

"Yes," Andrea said. "First, he got a shot, then there was the blue dream. And when he woke up, he could go home again."

"Mom is having her blue dream now," I said. "Let's sleep."

I woke up at dawn. The lights in the living room were still on. I went to the toilet. On my way back, I looked into our parents' bedroom. The bed was empty. I lay down on our mother's side and pressed my nose to her pillow. When I looked up, our father was standing next to the closet. I watched him getting dressed. Our mother must have watched him getting dressed a thousand of times. He sat down on his side of the bed to put on his shoes. Then he turned around and touched my shoulder. "You're going to be late for school."

I pretended to be asleep. He stroked my hair and then he lay down next to me. I didn't move. I felt his strong arms around me, and I heard the birds singing loudly next to the open window, and I wanted to say something that would make him laugh but I feared that he would get up and that I also would have to get up. "It'll be all right," he whispered time and again, but I knew it wasn't me he was talking to.

Our mother had stopped working at the library when she got pregnant with my brother. She sometimes did odd jobs for a friend, like typing letters or filling in forms, but she always worked at home. It was the first time that we were alone in the morning. We were having breakfast when our father had to leave for work. He looked at my brother. "Can you manage?"

Still chewing, Milan nodded.

"See you later," our father said.

I smiled at Andrea as I heard the door falling into the lock. "What do you want for lunch?" It was exciting to take care of ourselves for the first time. I imagined telling my friends at school later. I imagined telling them how I had prepared our lunchboxes.

"Nutella," Andrea said.

I went to fetch it from the shelf. Nutella was for weekends only. On weekdays, it was muesli, and our lunchboxes would be filled with apples and vegetables and cheese sandwiches. I opened the glass and dipped the knife into the dark brown mass. I spread it generously on the bread and then I dipped the knife back in and licked it off.

"Mommy will be mad," my sister said.

I shrugged. "She'll never know."

"Is she going to die?"

I looked at Milan.

He said, "She'll be out in a couple of days."

"How do you know?"

"Because Dad told me."

"What did he say?" Cutting another slice of bread I said, "What's wrong with mum?"

"Nothing." He refilled his cereal bowl and reached for the milk. "I'm staying home today."

"Are you crazy?"

He pointed at the clock. "We'd be late anyway."

"I'm going to tell Dad," I said.

"Don't you dare," my brother said.

Andrea looked at me. I shrugged. "We're all staying." I turned on the radio and said, "Daddy's going to take care of it." I smiled. "He'll talk to your teacher." Andrea was in fourth grade. Her last report hadn't been as good as ours; it was not a hundred percent sure that she would be admitted to the *Gymnasium*.

"When something has happened in the family, teachers are always nice." The mother of one of my classmates died in a car accident and he didn't have to write tests. The teachers sat down with him after school, some even took him home for lunch, and whenever he began to cry, he could sit in the headmaster's office eating sweets and reading comic books.

Andrea turned to our brother. "Why is she in hospital?"

He took a sharp knife out of the drawer and started punching it between his fingers. He'd become quite fast. I could often hear him practicing in his room.

"Why is she in hospital?" I asked.

Milan reached for the Nutella jar, closed it, put it onto the cupboard so that we couldn't reach it. "Stop asking me stupid questions, will you?"

He took out a book from his schoolbag and started reading, while we were listening to the radio, watching the clock above the sink, saying, "Now math is over," or, "I didn't do my homework anyway." At some point I took out my pencil case and Andrea made a drawing and I tried to write a letter to our mother but I didn't get farther than, *Hallo mum, how are you? We are all fine.* At noon, our brother went to the cabinet, took out a pot, filled it with water. "How about some pasta?" He lit a match and turned on the stove. "Watch Maestro Milan."

We watched him getting the olive oil from the sideboard. We watched him slice onions with the sharp knife and slide them into the pan. We watched him add a can of crushed tomatoes. We'd never seen our brother cook before, he must have practiced elsewhere. He rinsed the pasta through a sieve, and then he placed the pot on the table. Next to it, he put the pan with the tomato sauce. "Hand over your plates."

It looked perfect. A red circle in the middle surrounded by green tagliatelle. Like the dish my mother had in the restaurant on Easter Monday. I carefully rolled up the pasta with my fork and led it to my mouth. I blew, tried it, spat it out.

"What?" My brother stopped filling his own plate and said, "Spoiled little brat."

"It's too salty," I said.

Milan grabbed the salt and poured it into the sauce. He stirred it and then he held the spoon to my mouth. "Eat."

I shook my head.

He pressed the spoon between my lips. "Open Sesame," he said and I shook my head again. The sauce sprayed all over me.

"Look at you," my brother said, laughing.

I got up and reached for the dish towel. "What's wrong with you?"

"Can't you take a joke?"

I took my spoon, dipped it into the sauce and flipped it at him. "*Now* you got me laughing."

Andrea said, "I'm going to call Dad."

107

Milan got up and blocked the door. "You're not." He was standing there, bare-chested, in striped shorts. I dipped the spoon into the sauce again and flipped it at him. Milan didn't move. He watched me, grinning. I flipped and flipped.

When the pot was empty, I smiled at my sister. "Look at him now."

"I'm bleeding," he said, sinking to the ground. "You bitches killed me."

When our father returned from work, we were sitting in the living room, watching TV. We hadn't cleaned up the kitchen but he didn't call us. When the program was over, I got up, peeped through the door. I heard the radio playing softly and I heard the noise my mother usually made when she was doing the dishes. I went to the toilet, and when I came out again, my father was waiting for me. "How was your day?"

"Okay," I said.

"Fine," he said.

"When are we going to the hospital?"

My father handed me my unfinished letter. "Why don't you write a bit more? It'll make your mom very happy." He took Andrea's drawing from the table. "This too."

"I want to give it to her myself," I said.

He pulled me close, caressed my back, kissed me on the hair. "We'll go there soon."

The next morning, we woke up to the smell of scrambled eggs and bacon. There also was hot cocoa, in the jug we never used on ordinary days, because it was nearly eighty years old and already had a crack. "It feels like Sunday, doesn't it?" our father said. "Why, let's turn it into a Sunday." He called at school to say that we were sick and when we were done eating, he sent us to our rooms to get dressed. We went to the leisure park in Hamburg and ate candy floss and French fries. We rode the rollercoaster. Our father sat next to Andrea, and Milan and I followed right behind them. When we got to the highest point, Milan put his arm around me. "Don't throw up on my new jeans."

And I closed my eyes and put my head on his shoulder, waiting for my stomach to dance.

After a week, we were told that we couldn't go on like this. Milan stood up from his chair. He had become as tall as our father. He raised an eyebrow and said, "Go on like what?"

Our father rolled up his sleeves and started to do the dishes. "I called Aunt Sol," he said. "She'll be here tonight."

"Why?"

Our father reached for the kitchen towel and hung it over my brother's shoulder. "Because you need somebody to look after you, that's why."

"We don't," my brother said.

"You said that Mom would be back any day," I said.

"She will," our father said.

I piled up the plates and put them into the hot water. "When?"

"Soon," father said.

Milan looked at him. "As if."

In the evening our father went to the station to get Aunt Sol. We hadn't seen her in years. She lived only two hours away from us and had often said she would come for a visit, but something had always come in her way. She kissed us all, even my brother. She had brought two big suitcases and her cat. Our mother was allergic to cats.

Our father said, "We'll take everything to the drycleaners." He looked around. "We can move, too. We've been here too long anyway."

Andrea was already carrying the cat around the place. I said, "I'm not going to move."

Milan said, "How was your trip?"

Aunt Sol smiled. "Awful. I was put on a wagon full of eighth graders." She looked at me and smiled. "At least I'm up to date with the newest hair style."

"I'm in eighth grade," I said.

"I know you are, sweetie." Aunt Sol took a six-pack out of her bag, turned to our father, said, "I'd die for a beer."

He led her to the kitchen. I stayed in the hall. I could hear them talking softly, and I could hear my sister playing with the cat. I could hear the TV that Milan had turned on. I was leaning against the wall, looking at the clothes rack. After the Ice Saints our mother had put all the winter gear into blue plastic bags and stored them in the cellar, except for her navy-blue coat. "It might get cold again," she'd said. I took the coat down, brought it into my room, stuffed it under my blanket. My sister looked at me, saying, "What are you doing?" She was still carrying that cat in her arms.

"Nothing," I said.

She held the cat up to my face. "Do you want to hold her?"

I backed off. "If I catch it in my bed, I'll throw it out of the window."

My sister smiled. "She has nine lives."

I went to the window and opened it. "What if it's the last one?"

In the morning, Aunt Sol was already in the kitchen when I came to eat my cereals. Our father was gone. There were hot pancakes on the table, and there were three lunchboxes. I took a dirty bowl out of the sink.

110

"There are clean ones in the cabinet," Aunt Sol said.

I went to the kitchen cart to get the cereals. I went to the fridge to get the milk.

"There's milk on the table, honey," she said.

I looked at her feet. She was wearing Mom's clogs. "Why are you here?"

Aunt Sol smiled. "Your dad asked me to come," she said.

"Why?"

"He had been asking for years and I didn't want to put it off again." She turned around and said, "Good morning, sleepyhead."

My sister was pressing her doll to her chest. She hadn't played with that doll in years. "She wants her milk," she said, holding up the doll's bottle.

"Don't act like a baby," I said.

Aunt Sol bent down and caressed the doll's head. "She'll get it."

Andrea watched Aunt Sol while she heated up the milk and poured it into the doll's bottle. Then she passed her the doll and said, "You feed her."

Aunt Sol sat down and took the doll into her arms and pretended to feed her, but Andrea pushed the doll away, climbed onto Aunt Sol's lap, and began to whimper like a baby. Aunt Sol laughed and then led the bottle to my sister's mouth.

I grabbed my cereals to eat in my room. In the hall I ran into Milan who was standing in front of the mirror, combing his hair. I stopped short and spilled milk over his jacket. He slapped the bowl out of my hands. "You better watch it."

Aunt Sol came out of the kitchen, still carrying my sister. "I'll clean it," she said. "You get ready for school, honey."

I went to the bathroom to get toilet paper. Aunt Sol put

111

Andrea down and fetched a bucket and a scrub. "Let me do it," she said. "You're going to be late."

I continued unrolling the toilet paper until there was nothing to unroll anymore. Milan watched me shaking his head. "What's your fucking problem?"

Aunt Sol touched his shoulder and said, "Go get your lunchbox."

The whole floor was covered with toilet paper. I wrapped it around my head. When my eyes and my mouth were covered, I said, "I want Mom."

"I know, honey."

"I want my Mom," I said. "Now."

Andrea said, "You look like an Egyptian mummy."

"Don't touch me. Don't anybody dare touch me." I stood up and stretched out my arms to feel the way to my room where I tore off the toilet paper and got dressed.

That day I didn't go to school. I didn't get off the bus. I wanted to, I even got as far as the exit, and then I walked on to the last row and sat down next to an old woman who was holding a dog on her lap. She allowed me to caress him. "He's getting old," she said. "He can hardly walk anymore."

"What's his name?" I asked.

"Baldur." She patted the dog's head and said, "He was bold and brave once." She smiled. "I was too."

I felt the quick pounding of the dog's heart. He didn't seem to mind my touching him. He had thrown a quick glance at the old woman when I first laid my hand on his back, but now he'd accepted me.

"It's the old age," the woman said. "Makes you happy about the smallest sign of tenderness." She looked up. "Don't you have to go to school?"

"My mom's in hospital," I said. "I'm going to visit her."

"Sorry to hear that."

"It's nothing," I said. "She'll be out next week."

"She must be very happy to have such a beautiful daughter." She put the dog down on the floor and got up. "It was nice talking to you," she said. "Take care."

"You too," I said, caressing the dog for one last time. When she was gone, I realized that I didn't even know to which hospital they'd taken her.

After the school secretary had called our father to tell him that I hadn't shown up, he started taking us to school in his car. He waited until we all disappeared inside and I sat in class and nothing reached me, as if they were talking in a foreign language. The teachers looked at me, and I looked at them, at their lips opening and closing, until the school bell rang.

When we went down the stairs, my friend Linda offered to work with me in the afternoon or on weekends. We stepped onto the schoolyard and sat down on the bench under the walnut tree. I looked up at the branches loaded with ripe walnuts, hoping for them to fall on my head, hoping for them to rain down on me, to bury me.

Linda touched the sleeve of my mother's coat and said, "Aren't you hot?"

I shook my head.

She put her arm around me. "Nikki."

I grabbed my bag. "I forgot my book."

Aunt Sol stayed for another week. Then she had to go home to her boyfriend and her job. Andrea wouldn't stop crying until our aunt offered to take her and our father let her go. I didn't speak to him for days, until he said, "I'm taking you both to the hospital tomorrow."

When our mother came home, our father turned the living-room sofa into a bed. We ordered pizza or Chinese, or

113

Milan went to the Indian restaurant to get us dinner. We lay on the floor in front of the sofa and watched TV or played board games. We were taking turns in lying next to our mother. Milan went out only once because our mother insisted. When he kissed her good bye, she said, "You have fun, young man."

Our father took out his wallet and counted five bills. He pressed them into Milan's hand. "Listen to your mom, will you?"

Our father lifted Andrea and let her sit on his lap, feeding her the baby bottle that Aunt Sol had bought. I put on a record by Ella Fitzgerald, which was our mother's favourite, and lay down next to her on the sofa, and she covered me with the warm blanket and held me until I fell asleep.

Then she was gone again. Andrea went back to Aunt Sol. Milan had a girlfriend now. I saw them in the park once. She sat with her back against a chestnut tree, and he was telling her something, making gestures with his hands. They didn't stop laughing. I walked up to them and said, "How can you just sit here?"

The girl looked at Milan. "Do you know her?"

He raised an eyebrow. "Beat it."

"Did you even tell her?"

"What happened to your hair?" He smirked. "You should have used a trimmer."

His girlfriend said, "Who is she?"

"Why are you wearing that coat? It's summer in case you didn't get it." Milan touched my shoulder and said, "You really look stupid."

I pushed him away. "Leave me alone."

He took my hand and held it tight. "Stop that."

I felt a wall of tears pushing against my eyes. "Mom is

114

dying and you're sitting here as if there was nothing."

He tightened his grip. "She's not."

I sank down next to him and buried my face in his T-shirt and he put his arms around me and said, "Stop crying, will you?" He pressed his mouth to my hair and said, "Please."

I couldn't. But he couldn't either.

I read that praying could help, so I closed my eyes and said, "Please, let her come home tomorrow." I hid my folded hands under my coat and lowered my head. "If she comes home tomorrow I will do anything." I should have offered something but there was nothing I could think of.

Milan started coming home late at night. In the beginning he was quiet, but after a while he didn't seem to care anymore if he woke us up. I heard his loud steps as he went to the kitchen. I heard him opening the fridge. I heard him burp. I was waiting for our father to come out of the living room, but he never did. He was sleeping on the sofa now. Sometimes, I slept in our parent's bed, on our mother's side. Our father still drove us to school, but he didn't wait for us to go in anymore. Milan sat down on one of the benches in the hall, saying, "See you later." When I looked at him from the top of the stairs, he still sat there, eyes closed, as if asleep. Eventually one of the teachers would tell him to get going. Or they would not. It was difficult to talk to him these days.

When I showed up in class, the teachers always smiled at me. They never said that I was too late. Then there was a new teacher. She said, "Who are you?"

I went to my desk. I took out my book and my folder.

"Tell me your name," the new teacher said.

I rummaged through my bag for a pen, and when I

looked up again, she stood in front of my desk. She leaned toward me. "What's the matter with you?"

I stared at the map that was hanging on the wall. I read the names of the countries and memorized them. Even today, I can still see the map if I close my eyes, and the names of the countries: Morocco, Algiers, Tunisia. I can still see the stains on the wall, in all kinds of colours. "My mother died last night," I said.

The new teacher put a hand on my back. "I'm so sorry."

I heard the others breathe in. I heard them sigh. I felt warm and comfortable, with the new teacher's hand on my back. I lowered my head and said, "She had cancer."

The headmaster called to give his condolences while I was watching TV. I heard our father talking on the telephone. Then he came into the living room and opened the sideboard. He took one of the bottles, filled a glass, sat down next to me on the carpet. "That was your headmaster. He wanted to know where to send flowers."

I bit on my lip. Then I said, "What did you say?"

"I told him to make a donation to Greenpeace."

"Really?"

"No," he said. "I told him that we're all out of our minds at the moment." He put his hand on my shoulder and said, "She will make it."

I continued watching TV, but he didn't leave and he didn't remove his hand from my shoulder, so I said, "I don't know why I said that. I really don't know."

That night Milan pissed against the clothes rack. I ran into the hall because I heard our father shouting, "Stop it." Milan was pressing a bottle of wine to his chest, and he was singing, "Where is my mind?" Our father stepped forward and took the bottle away. "Where is my mind? Where is my

116

mind?" my brother went on. "It's okay, son," our father said and he put his arms around Milan and Milan started to cry like a baby and our father rocked him back and forth. I waited for a while, but they didn't look up, so I returned to my room and tried to read, until my father sat down next to me. I put my arms around him and he sighed and I felt all the air streaming out of him and for a moment, I was afraid that he would deflate like a balloon, but then he straightened up again and hugged me back and turned out the light and held my hand until I fell asleep.

Then she came home for good. We didn't talk about the treatments and the months that were behind us. Milan's girlfriend was studious, and he tried to keep up with her. Andrea invented reasons to miss school, and our mother let her. Often, when I came home, they were lying on the sofa, listening to music, and they hardly looked up when I said hello.

In the evening, our mother cooked dinner for us but somehow she had forgotten how hungry we always were and there was never enough. She looked at the empty pots and pans frowning, and my father laughed and put a frozen pizza into the oven or he sent us to the ice-cream parlour. After doing the dishes together they often went for a walk. I saw them on the other side of the street once and the sight of her in the navy-blue coat, which seemed much too large for her now, made me turn around and run until I was back downtown where a row of little cardboard cars in all kinds of colours asthmatically clattered along the streets. They moved as slowly as a funeral procession, emitting clouds of reeking blue fumes. People sitting in the cars cheered and waved, and people seaming the street cheered and waved too, and put coins and bananas onto the hoods.

I sat down on the stairs of an apartment house to wait

for the end of the line in order to cross the street but there were more and more coming. A man, whose haircut and clothes looked funny, passed me a banana, saying, "The wall came down. They tore down the fucking wall."

When I came home it was long after midnight but our mother, who had wrapped one arm around my sleeping sister, just looked up from her book and smiled and said, "Are you okay, love?"

I knew that she was waiting for me to kiss her good-night, but I didn't, I turned around and closed the door and went to my room where I sank onto my bed and fell asleep immediately, in my clothes, shoes and all.

Floating

It was her first home visit. She looked up at the thoroughly renovated apartment house and lit a cigarette, tossed it away after a few quick puffs and searched her pockets for the roll of mints. After she'd thrown a handful into her mouth, she rang the doorbell.

"Top floor," the mother said over the intercom.

Sophie opened her bag and produced a bottle of water, which she finished in one go while waiting next to the elevator. The fully mirrored cage's lighting was merciless. She kept her eyes shut until it stopped ascending. When it finally released her, she knocked on a half-closed door and opened it. The mother approached her, holding a French press. "Good morning, Mrs. Wittgenstein. That is really so nice of you. Hopefully you didn't have to postpone your Christmas plans."

Sophie wiped her boots on the doormat. It had a floral design, blending with the words: *Home Sweet Home*. She'd never bought a doormat. She would always think about getting one, but then it was time to move again. "I don't live far. No bother at all."

"Well," the mother said. "Come on in."

Sophie stepped inside. The coats hung neatly on the rack, above a shelf in which woman's and boy's shoes were properly placed. A typical hall of a typical family, she'd say, apart from the fact that the father was absent.

"Can you please take off your boots?"

Sophie looked down on them. They weren't dirty anymore. Could she refuse? She looked up again.

The mother held up the press. "Or would you rather like tea?"

"Coffee is fine," Sophie said, bending forward to unzip her left boot.

119

In the beginning they had been paying these visits to every single student, one of her colleagues had told her. Not anymore, the school had become much too big and popular, but homeroom teachers were still encouraged to do so, especially in the case of a student in need of special attention. At the last conference all of her colleagues had agreed that her student Vincent belonged to that category. "I don't think that's right," Sophie said.

Everybody stared at her. The math teacher, who'd begun a month after her, said, "Why not?"

"I'd feel like someone from the *Stasi*."

The head put her hand on hers and said, "Not at all. It's because we care. Not to control but to understand and to help."

Sophie hadn't dared to refuse anymore and she hadn't dared to ask how such a visit was supposed to be. She still hoped that the mother would find a way to prevent her intrusion, but hardly an hour after sending the email she got a positive answer, even though she'd proposed to come by the day before Christmas Eve. Before leaving her place she'd checked her mails hoping that the whole thing would be called off; she'd even considered calling it off herself, but there would be an extra meeting right after the holidays to discuss her report.

"This way," the mother said.

Sophie recognized items she'd seen in the IKEA catalogue, like the rug for example, which she'd wanted to buy, but when she finally had the money, it was sold out. That was the main reason why she'd applied for the job; she'd longed to stop worrying about money.

The mother filled their cups with coffee. They had a complete set, of course. Sophie's father had tried to give her one of their sets for years but she was fine with the few ill-matched dishes she had. No harm done if something broke, she would have less to pack when she had to move again. She liked moving; she started searching the internet the moment a place became depressing.

"Please have a seat," the mother said.

Sophie sank onto the sofa and took out a folder. "We thought that it might be good to meet in a familiar setting."

The mother looked into her eyes.

"It's the procedure at our school," Sophie went on. "To visit our students at home, I mean."

"That is so nice of you," the mother said.

In the corner there was a swing cradle. When they decided to move together the first thing they must have done was go to IKEA, the mother heavily pregnant, the father-to-be caring and all, that place full of people like them. Sophie always imagined them breaking up again, fighting over dented dishes or torn furniture, or what was even worse, generously offering the whole lot to the other to get something more exquisite, more solid, for the next, better home.

The mother smiled. "Milk? Sugar?"

Sophie had been living in Berlin for maybe a year when she sat in a café with a friend and they'd looked at the façades of the apartment houses, imagining the people behind the windows, families sitting at dinner tables, men beating women (or the other way round, her friend pointed out), teenagers feeling ugly and superfluous, lonely grown-ups next to empty wine bottles, toddlers crying for parents who wanted them to get used to loneliness. Fifty shades of horror, her friend had whispered, more to himself than to Sophie. "Yes, please," she said to her host now.

The son came into the room. Neatly dressed, hair combed, straight posture. Bare feet as usual. He didn't salute, but still resembled a soldier. Yes, she thought, he reminds me of Grimms' tin soldier. Or was it Andersen?

121

She cleared her throat. "Good morning, Vincent," she said. "We are a little bit worried."

The mother said, "Why?"

Sophie cleared her throat again. "Can I have a glass of water, please?"

"Go get a glass of water for your teacher, honey." The son leaped out of the room and his mother looked at Sophie frowning, "Are you all right, Miss Wittgenstein?"

"I'm fine." Sophie had difficulties in reading her colleagues' notes. She looked up and took the glass of water from the son. "He never mentioned the baby." She drank up and said, "How old?"

"Five weeks," the mother said.

Sophie tried to remember what she'd planned to say: he only wore sandals regardless of the time of year (no socks!), always kept to himself even if they had to work in pairs, always sat in the farthest corner, never said a word, not in class, not at lunch, not on the rare occasions when they were out of school. He was so quiet that she'd accidentally locked him up in the classroom once. "Has Vincent been tested?"

"Tested?"

"Medical examinations turned out okay?" She cleared her throat again. She'd smoked too much. Far too much. She should pause for a while, at least for today. "It's the procedure. We'll have to ask all the parents just to make sure." The last time she'd suggested that a kid wasn't behaving normally she'd been cited to the headmaster's office to listen to a long speech on the uniqueness of every human being.

"Of course," the mother said.

The son was still smiling, maybe he wasn't listening. His gaze seemed full of attention but he never blinked and his pupils never moved, like the eyes of a doll they had tried to construct as real as possible. She had such a doll once, a very expensive doll given to her by a great-aunt, but she couldn't sleep with these eyes watching her, so her parents took it away.

"It's just a routine visit," Sophie said.

The mother fiddled with her pony tail that nearly reached her hips. No trace of grey. She had to be around Sophie's age and yet, she already had two kids. Sophie sat straight. She was the teacher, she reminded herself, ergo to be respected. Hadn't she herself wondered at the last parents' evening how they'd looked at her? Not only respectful but vulnerable in a way? Hanging on her lips, pondering every word she said? Waiting patiently afterward to talk to her one-to-one, be it only for a minute? She wished people would listen to her like this in real life.

"Vincent never said that there were any problems," the mother said.

"We just want to make sure that he feels okay, at school, that is…" Sophie stopped, looked at the son, then at his mother again. "He's always alone."

The mother smiled. "There are people who have a lot of friends, and there are others who like to be on their own. People from the second category aren't necessarily unhappy."

"Team work is important at our school," Sophie said.

The mother put an arm around the son who'd pulled up his knees and slung his skinny arms around them. He looked so small; nobody would believe that he was twelve years old. "Team work is important everywhere."

Outside, it had begun to snow. They would have a white Christmas, Sophie's father had said, when she'd called him to say that she would stay in Berlin this year. It was the first time that she wouldn't come home for Christmas, and if her mother were still alive, she wouldn't feel so bad now, but at the age of thirty-five, she'd told herself, one should be allowed to make plans without asking permission. She wanted to sleep in, no plans, no obligations. Maybe she would fly away for a couple of days, to some place with warm sand instead of cold snow. Now that she could afford such things. She nodded toward the son's naked feet. "Aren't you cold?"

He looked down at his tiny toes. Then he looked up again and said, "No."

Sophie finished her coffee. "The PE teacher only saw him once."

"Is that true, Vincent?"

"I was there every time, Mom."

Sophie closed the folder. "I'm just repeating what my colleagues said."

"I totally trust my son," the mother said. "If he says he was there, he was."

A colleague had told Sophie that they'd caught an eighth grader with a big bag of grass on a class trip. His parents were convinced that someone had played a trick on him. That kid got away scot-free in the end. A month before she'd seen a group of tenth graders buying vodka and cigarettes. She was supposed to address them and inform their parents even if it was on the weekend. "You're a teacher 24/7," her boss had told the newcomers. "Teaching isn't the main thing we do here, it's education." Like the others Sophie had dutifully nodded but when she saw the students she quickly turned around and waited behind the cereal shelves until they had disappeared. Since then she'd made it a habit to do her shopping on Saturday mornings, when the kids were still young and accompanied by their parents. Sophie suppressed a yawn. "Just make sure that the teachers check your name in the future, will you?"

"It can be quite chaotic in a gym with all the kids

running around. Must be hard to distinguish one from the other, don't you think?" The mother stood up and opened the door to a cabinet. She came back with a photograph showing Vincent and a man in running gear. "That's Vincent and his father at the Hamburg Marathon. He didn't run the whole distance of course, but he got quite far." She had a closer look at the photograph, as if she herself hadn't seen it before, then wiped over it with her sleeve before putting it on the table. "He's small for his age, but with boys everything's possible. There was a guy in my class, he was always the smallest, and at graduation he was a head taller than all of us." She refilled Sophie's cup and said, "Vincent's father is tall too. Just give him time."

The man looked familiar but people in sports gear all looked alike, didn't they? Sophie opened the folder again. She should at least make some notes. Pen ready she said, "Is there anything else we should know?"

"What do you mean?"

"For some kids it's quite hard to suddenly have to share their parents."

The mother turned to her son. "You like being the big brother, don't you?"

The son nodded the way he always nodded when Sophie was talking to him. Sometimes, he didn't seem to understand anything she said. Sometimes, she even asked him to repeat what she'd said, which he did, like a parrot, as if he had no idea what her words meant.

"What about his father?" Sophie said.

The mother said, "Vincent spends every other weekend with him."

"And the father of the baby?" Sophie cleared her throat again and said, "Does he get along with Vincent?"

The mother looked at the cradle. "Some people would call it an accident, for us it's a miracle."

125

Sophie rubbed her temples to make the throbbing go away. She'd told Hugo that she had to work in the morning and would have to go to bed shortly, just one beer, she'd said and he'd said okay, but in the end she fell asleep at 6.30, the time when her alarm clock went off on work days, surrounded by empty beer bottles and full ashtrays. Usually she met friends at bars or cafés. She was fine with people telling her about their problems but preferred not to be shown. Fucking though was something one had to do at home and since Hugo lived with his girlfriend it had to be Sophie's apartment. When she was younger she avoided taking men home but in the end she came to appreciate staying in bed while the other had to get out of it in the middle of the night. She remembered these nights with horror, when she stepped out of unknown apartment houses, onto unknown streets in unknown neighbourhoods, not having any clue where to find a night bus or the next subway station.

"I grew up with three siblings," the mother said. "There was always somebody at home." She nodded toward her son, who stood up and left, then she said, "I know a lot of women who wanted to wait for the right moment. But then it was too late. Or it never came."

The central heating was blowing warm air into Sophie's direction. She took off her sweater and still felt hot. Her apartment was freezing because she'd forgotten to order briquettes.

The mother leaned forward and touched her underarm. "Mrs. Wittgenstein?"

Sophie got up, looked out the window, said, "I better be going." The snow would melt soon, it would become dirty slush sticking to her boots, but at her father's it would soften her steps and turn the landscape into a white sheet. He'd barely been able to hide his disappointment when

126

she'd said that she had piles of tests to correct (which was a lie).

The mother stepped up next to her. "I love winter," she said. "When it's snowing outside, with all of us comfy indoors."

Sophie approached the cradle. Attached to its hood was a mobile, a set of fairies, thirteen altogether; no one would feel left out and cast a spell on this baby. She couldn't see its head though – the blanket had been pulled up. Just a tiny hand was peeking out. "She's sleeping like a log."

"It's a boy." The mother reached for the baby's hand. "Do you have children?"

"No."

The mother looked at her but said nothing.

Sophie turned around and grabbed the folder. "Why is Vincent wearing sandals in winter?" She picked up her sweater and said, "And no socks. How can he run around with no socks in winter?"

"I told him time and again. He says his feet can't breathe." The mother bent down to kiss the baby's hand. "You stop wondering after a while. That's what family is for, to accept the others the way they are."

"Doesn't always work out, does it?"

"My husband is a good father, that's all I care for nowadays."

Most probably he'd left them for another woman. Sophie didn't pity her; she should have known better. They all didn't want to know. For the sake of their holy family. She'd once seen a friend's boyfriend with another girl. She told her friend and gave her comfort and tried to distract her. In the end the boyfriend apologized and the two got back together and Sophie had become the one to blame. "You're just jealous," her friend had said. "What do you know about relationships?" Maybe it was the only way to

127

stay close together. Keep eyes and ears shut. One just had to look at these mothers who defended their sons no matter what they'd done. She shoved the folder into her bag. "Let me just say good-bye to him."

The kitchen door was ajar. On the table there were the remains of breakfast and a folded newspaper. A woollen blanket hung over the back of the bench. She pictured mother and son sitting there not too long ago, still in their night clothes, spreading butter on a warm croissant, a steaming cup in front of them. She could hear the mother saying, "Get dressed, honey. Your teacher's coming soon. So close to Christmas, isn't that strange? Maybe she doesn't have family."

The mother opened a door. "Say good-bye to your teacher, hon."

Sophie stepped forward. "This is a nice room." There were French windows leading to a huge terrace on which the snow had turned everything white already. As if someone had covered chairs and loungers and tables with blankets, like in these films about families who leave their mansion by the sea to return to the city after the summer holidays, not knowing if they would ever return. Vincent crouched next to a huge *Playmobil* school. There was a small classroom, a gym, and a computer lab. In front of it, mothers and fathers bringing their kids to school, waving after them as they walk to the entrance door carrying books and schoolbags. Sophie joined him. She carefully placed the tiny globe onto the tiny desk and grabbed the teacher figure. "Good morning everybody," she said in a high voice. "Which of you can show me Africa?"

The son frowned.

"We had to put it up one more time to take pictures." The mother was pressing the baby to her torso now. Its face was turned toward her; it still didn't move or make a sound. "Vincent wants to sell it on eBay."

"He is so quiet," Sophie said. "Like his brother."

"He wasn't when he was born." The mother stroked the son's head. "He was a hard nut really. Keeping us up all night, weren't you?" She laughed and said, "His father had to carry him around all night."

On the wall next to the bed there was a large photo showing a man with a baby carrier, face turned in. "Unfortunately he had to move to Hamburg," the mother said. "But Vincent loves the train rides. He's been doing it on his own since he turned nine." The mother looked at the son and then turned back to Sophie. "There are jobs you can't say no to. He's an architect."

Sophie stepped forward to have a closer look. She knew that man. They'd met at a party. He'd told everybody that he would have the run of the house for a couple of weeks because wife and son had gone for a visit to the in-laws. They got drunk on Mojito that night, kissed, and when it was dawning, he took her home and straight to the bedroom where he split a pill and put one half on Sophie's tongue. Swallowing the other half, he pushed her on the bed. She remembered that it was getting dark as she stepped outside again. "Where is the bedroom?"

"The bedroom?"

"We had this case once." She shrugged. "The kid's room and the living-room were in perfect shape, but they'd piled up all the mess in the bedroom."

The mother blushed. "Is this the reason why you're here?"

Sophie smiled apologetically. "I'll be out in a minute."

The mother opened the remaining door. This was the room Sophie had been taken from that night. This was the bed. The sheets that landed on the floor, soaked with their sweat and fluids. The carpet covered with clothes reeking of cigarettes. The night table from which they'd knocked their wine glasses. The bare mattress full of ash and stains. The French windows leading to the snow covered terrace where they'd sunbathed naked that day.

"I know who you are," the mother said.

Sophie turned around.

"Don't worry. He didn't leave because of you. There were others."

The baby started to cry.

"I have to feed him," the mother said.

Sophie pressed the bag against her chest, the bag that she'd bought for work and wouldn't use for anything else, in which she carried around things that had nothing to do with her life. "I didn't know that he was married."

"And if you knew you wouldn't have?" The mother sat down on the bed. "I had a friend who only slept with married men. Because they don't make demands. Her exact words. Do you think so too?"

Sophie reached out for the sideboard. Something concrete to hold on to. All these thick carpets everywhere, they made one feel unstable and insecure. She should have left her boots on. "I'll find my own way out," she said. "Merry Christmas."

The mother unbuttoned her blouse, uncovered her breast, and gave it to her baby. Sophie stared at them while the rhythmic sucking noise echoed from wall to wall. For a while the mother seemed to have forgotten that she had a visitor, then she looked up again and said, "You can't hurt us. Not then, not now."

The baby stopped sucking and looked at Sophie with distrust. She hurried out of the room, grabbed her coat and boots, and fled.

Bremen, Ohio

I'd begun to ask myself, How did I get here? but I hadn't yet realized that I was already on my way home. A man with a cowboy hat pointed to a sign saying: 'No self-service' and then filled my Coupe de Ville. He asked me where I came from.

"San Jose," I said.

"That's a long way, young lady."

It was pointless to tell him that my way had been much longer. Instead, I waited for him to praise my car. More than twenty years old, it still looked like new. He started to clean the windshield and said, "Better get new wipers."

I remembered how I first sank onto the red leather upholstery and how my hands held the wheel and how my foot pushed down the gas. "They're gonna love it in the East," I said.

He laughed and I paid. Then I went to the diner on the other side of the road and ordered a double-cheese and a beer. The waitress asked me whether I was from East or West Germany. The Wall had been history for two years. Nevertheless, I answered, "From the West."

A woman sat down next to me and said in German, "Me, too."

My heart skipped a beat. I hadn't heard my mother tongue for such a long time. "Really?"

She smiled as if I'd just shared a secret with her, then she said, "It isn't like driving from Flensburg to Munich, is it?"

"Right," I said even though highways all around the world are just grey lines that never end.

To make things short: her name was Karen, and she offered me a place to stay for the night. In her pick-up she led me along a dirt road and I thought about all those stories and movies where that wasn't a good idea. After what seemed like ages, she stopped, got out, and lightly closed the door. "Our little house in the prairie," she said as I was getting out of my car.

We sat on the porch to have a last beer. Above us the sky dripped with stars. Karen asked me if I liked it here.

"You mean your place?"

She grinned. "I mean the States."

I thought of the first couple of months when I'd felt so free I'd forgotten my birthday. But that seemed like a long time ago. "I get lonely sometimes," I said.

She had taken off her cowboy boots and put her feet onto the table. "Don't you have a sweetheart?"

"I got two," I said, "one here and one over there."

I was meant to meet Ben at his parents' house in Baltimore the next evening. I'd told him that it was an old dream of mine to drive from the West to the East. "Usually, it's the other way round," he'd said, grinning.

Karen lit a cigarillo. "Then you haven't met the right one yet." She watched the smoke and said, "What are you waiting for?"

I tried to remember what she'd told me about her husband at the diner, other than that he'd died from cancer three years ago. "Waiting's just a bad habit," I said.

She got up and returned with two more beers. "How old are you?"

"Twenty-two."

A German shepherd came out of nowhere and sat next to her. Observing me, it lay down beneath her chair. "She is just shy," Karen said and opened the bottles on the porch fence. "I was twenty-two when I came here. Then I met Ray. You can guess the rest."

I couldn't but nodded anyway. "Don't you have kids?"

She shrugged. "We were on the road all the time, then we were getting used to having a real home, and when I started thinking about it, Ray came back from the doctor's."

The beer caps had left little marks in the wood, as if a child had sunk its teeth into it. "You still can have some," I said.

She chuckled. "Aren't you afraid?" she asked after a while.

The night before two teenage boys had jumped onto the roof of my car while I was trying to catch some sleep in a parking lot. I climbed onto the driver's seat, turned the key, hit the gas. Through the rear-view mirror I could see them rolling in the dirt as I was racing back toward the main road. "No," I said.

"It's a big country," Karen said. "You easily get lost."

I remembered how lost I had felt in little Germany and asked her if she ever got homesick.

"Ten years ago we were over there, me and Ray. After a few days we went nuts." She shooed away the cat that had been lying on a box in the corner and took a blanket out of it. She looked at my bare legs. "Nights are getting colder now."

The only jeans I hadn't cut off were buried deep down in my backpack. Unwashed. "You really live in the middle of nowhere," I said. "What if someone robs you?"

She pointed to the shotgun that was leaning against the wall like a broom. "Don't worry, I haven't touched it in years." Then she wanted to know if I would like to see the stables. I was happy enough to be sitting on the porch but the way she was looking at me made me get up again.

"Loneliness expresses the pain of being alone and solitude expresses the glory of being alone," she said, undoing her hair. "Paul Tillich said that. He was German, too."

I'd never heard that name, but I could have listened to her for hours. Two days ago Ben and I had our first fight. I didn't have a chance. I couldn't keep looking at the dictionary, could I?

Touching and petting the animals, Karen went ahead of me. She told me stories about each one: about her horse, about her husband's horse, about the pigs. The oldest sow was supposed to go to the butcher's the following day. "She's had a good life," Karen said. "What about you? Any future plans?"

I thought about Ben and his proposal. Over the last days I had tried to see myself working here, with kids going to school, and Ben sleeping next to me every night. "Taking a bath," I said.

Karen laughed, and after a pause she said that she could use some help. She would pay me, room and board included. Tony hadn't been well since Ray died, I could take care of him. It took me some time until I understood that she was talking about the horse.

"300 a week?" she said.

I said, "Way too much."

She winked at me. "There's plenty of work here. You're not going to drink that beer on my porch for free no more."

I wouldn't mind having arms like her. "How's the winter here?"

Karen bolted the stable doors and looked at the sky. I bet she could name every one of the stars. "Not as long as yours," she said.

The day before leaving San Jose I had gone to the beach. While Ben was at work. I sat down next to the sea and read a book I had brought with me from Germany. I'd like to think that it was Rilke, but it could just as well have been a

134

stupid detective story. At some point I began reading aloud. It was great to listen to my voice being that fluent. Next to me there was a couple. The girl came over and said in broken German that she had been studying at *Freie Universität*. She couldn't believe that I'd never been to Berlin. "It must be awesome," she said, "now that the Wall came down."

I followed Karen across the yard. We went past the vegetable garden and came to an old trailer. She turned on the lights. There was a Pullman kitchen, a table and two chairs, a couch and a king-size bed. There was even a small TV. "We don't have one at the house. Ray and I came here when we wanted to know what was happening in the world." She looked at the couch and said, "I'll bring you some fresh sheets."

I sunk onto the mattress. "My sleeping bag'll do just fine."

A bed just for myself. The first months I had given lessons in French and German to pay the rent, but then one pupil after the other had cancelled, and I had been happy enough to stay at Ben's. "I don't even know where I am."

Karen touched the map which was hanging on the wall. "We're here," her finger moved up one inch, "that's Dresden," then further to the left, "Hanover," then down again, "Bremen."

In the other Bremen, on the other side of the world, there was my boyfriend, and he would never leave it.

Karen opened the door. "We could have lots of fun." Her dog was waiting for her on the stairs. It didn't come in. It knew that she would be back in a while.

"Definitely," I said. We would take the horses for a ride. On Saturday evening we would hang about at the diner. I would dance with a lonely cowboy and let him beat me at pool. My gaze fell at a framed photograph. "Is that you?"

"It was taken three months after I arrived here." She smiled and said, "On the day I was supposed to take the plane back home." She laughed. "I was so young."

I sat on the bed, took off my worn-down chucks.

She reached under the bed and pulled out a box with cowboy boots. "You can't run around here in those."

"It's all I have," I said. "They are fine."

"You don't want them horses stepping on your toes." She smiled. "You don't want anyone to step on your toes."

I tried them all and ended up with some red ones. Blue seams.

"Much better," she said. "It's the first thing I bought when I came here."

I took them off again, stretched out on the bed. "Do you have a phone?"

"Sure."

"My boyfriend is waiting for me in Baltimore." I would ask him to come by. It would all be different. I'd have a home and a job. My English would get better, and I wouldn't be searching for words anymore.

"Back then we took our trailer everywhere," Karen said, running her finger along the shelf as if to check if it needed cleaning. "When we didn't like a place anymore, we just hit the road."

There was a Polaroid of a man with long hair and a beard on the door of the fridge. I said, "That's him, right?" It was two o'clock in the morning when I crawled into my sleeping bag. The moon peeped through the window, shone on my new boots. I saw myself wearing them, sitting on the old tractor that I'd seen in the drive. I saw myself writing a letter to my parents, telling them that I would stay. I saw myself writing another letter to my boyfriend in Bremen.

When I woke up it was still dark outside. Coming out of the trailer I could see my breath. I went to my car and opened the trunk to get the sweater that I'd last worn on the plane heading toward L.A.

Some time ago, our daughter and her boyfriend went down to the basement to check if there was anything for their new place in Berlin. They came back carrying the antique nightstand I'd been planning to bring to the restorer for years. My daughter unlocked the door. "Look at that," she said, holding up one of my red boots. She slipped into it, slipped out of it again, reached inside, and produced a folded piece of paper.

"Give it to me," I said.

She grinned. "Is it a love letter?"

"Don't be so cheeky." I unfolded it, read Karen's words: "I wish you a happy trip and a happy life." I found it under my wipers that early morning I drove back to the gas station to brush my teeth and have a cup of coffee. The man with the cowboy hat again warned me about the wipers and I ignored him again to find myself on the narrow, slippery streets of NYC in the middle of the same night, sticking out my head to see the cars up front, with the rain pouring down on me like a waterfall.

"Cool," my daughter said, "Can I have them?"

I looked up. She was standing in front of the mirror, wearing my red boots. She turned from one side to the other, looked at my boots from every angle, and then she turned to her boyfriend and said, "What do you think?"

"No," I said.

She looked at me the through the mirror, with her right eyebrow raised, and her upper lip slightly curled. "You're not going to wear cowboy boots at your age, are you?"

"You can have the nightstand," I said.

My boyfriend's daughter bent down and said, "One of the legs will come off soon."

She sat on the floor. "So what? Can't you repair that damn thing or what?"

I watched her taking off the boots, and I picked them up and pressed them to my stomach. The leather had gotten a bit hard but a bit of polish was all they needed. I watched my daughter and her boyfriend discussing whether to take a piece of furniture to their new home or not. I watched them thinking, I wish you a happy trip and a happy life.

The Accident

Vivien looked at the muscular legs of the runner who had just passed her. Soon he would disappear around the corner. Only a few years ago she'd been as fast as him. Sometimes Bernd had joined her, but after two rounds he'd given up and sat down on a bench to wait for her. And she kept on running, feeling strong, invincible, as if her legs could take her across town for hours if she wished so. But Doc Melzer had said that running wasn't good for her knees anymore. Otherwise she'd make it to a hundred, he'd added grinning.

Again someone passed her, this time a woman with a dangling ponytail. Her legs looked also strong and reliable and the distance between them grew within seconds, but then she suddenly slipped and fell. Vivien couldn't refrain from grinning. The woman would survive. At worst a scar would remind her of the pain.

Vivien unlocked the front door. Today she had to open the letterbox; she couldn't go on pretending to be on holiday. She looked at the pile in her hands (all directed to Bernd Adamski), fought the urge to throw everything into the waste paper container, and walked up to the fourth floor, slowing down with every step ("An elevator?" she'd said ten years ago, "Who the hell needs an elevator?"). In the silent apartment she opened and scanned the letters: bills, advertisement for a new spa, a note from the house management: the apartments were put on sale. They would have to pay 434,000 euros or move out.

She called her daughter Kristin and listened to her excuses why they wouldn't make it to Berlin for the time being. After passing her on to the grandchildren, who rattled off the usual (friends, school, the things Mommy and Daddy were refusing to buy), Kristin was back, distracted, impatient, eager to end the call. Vivien mentioned the letter from the house management. "We'll buy," she said and quickly hung up.

She took off her new running shoes (the sales clerk had looked at her sceptically when she'd asked for his advice; he even had the gall to ask if they were meant for her) and checked if the green light of the answering machine was blinking. She had made it a habit to leave her cell phone at home when she went running. One hour off a day, Doc Melzer had prescribed. "Why?" Vivien asked, expecting his hundred-year-theory, but he just smiled and said, "'Cause I say so."

She had a cup of tea in the kitchen. Bernd was the aficionado. To her the cheap brew coming in bags for 59ct served just as well. On her last birthday, he'd covered her eyes with a scarf and led her to their car. It nearly took them half an hour until he opened the passenger door and took her by the hand, saying, "Mind the curb," or "Careful!" She still wasn't allowed to look when he paid the entrance fee but then they were walking on gravel and after a few steps some of it had come into her shoes, so he finally took off the damned scarf: they were in a Japanese garden, after that she had to visit a Korean garden and after that a Chinese garden where Bernd had arranged a tea ceremony in a chintzy traditional hut. An Asian woman in a red dress with a fire-spitting dragon filled hot water into tiny cups, and Vivien had to taste again and again, and she had to pretend that the flavour changed every time even though it remained the same dishwater. Her feet were aching and she was dressed far too warmly, but when Bernd asked her if she'd liked it and she returned his gaze, she realized that she hadn't noticed the small brown spot at the rim of his right iris for much too long.

She opened the fridge and reached for the piece of

140

Gouda, put some butter onto a fluffy slice of bread, forced herself to eat. Bernd would shrink back with disgust. A few years ago he'd begun to bake bread himself. She could picture him now, standing in front of the oven with a pot cloth, looking at the clock; soon he would open the door, take the bread out, put it onto the tray and grab the knife, but then he would pause and they both would watch the steam rising into the air.

She left the half-finished sandwich on the plate she'd been using for three days at least, reached for her book, scanned a page, browsed a few pages back, started from the beginning, put the book back onto the table. The sun was hitting on the dried-out flowerpots. Early March they would always go to the store to buy soil and a variety of seeds and Bernd would carry the heavy bag up to their apartment and she would clear the table, place the pots next to each other, fill them with the still damp soil. She would carefully distribute the seeds while Bernd sat next to her, sipping tea, reading the newspaper. He'd also carried the bag up to the apartment seven years ago, when he was in love with that pathetic woman he'd met in the library, he drank his tea and read his newspaper while she cried although she'd forbidden herself to do that, because a face covered with tears was the last thing to get a husband back. Now it was nearly May and the pots were still carrying last year's soil, and last year's flowers were long gone, and there would be no new soil, no new flowers this year.

She went to the bathroom to wash her hands. On the sideboard there was the untouched bag with the make-up items she'd bought last week, after a heavily made-up assistant at *Kaufhof* had offered to do her face. At first she wanted to refuse, but then she thought that it would be a nice surprise for Bernd. She herself was surprised when she looked at the result in the mirror, to such a degree that she

141

found herself at the check-out with foundation, mascara, and eye shadow, everything by Helena Rubinstein, everything fucking expensive.

Bernd hadn't noticed of course. Or if he had, he'd shown no sign. Well. He just had to come home. They would drink his special tea and eat his home-made bread. She'd kept his after shave and his electric tooth brush. His bathrobe was hanging next to the towels, freshly washed. His massage oil was standing next to his antiperspirant stick. All she had to do was to get rid of the dust. All she had to do was give the whole place a good thorough cleaning.

She was just putting on her coat when the doorbell rang. After some hesitation she said into the intercom, "Hello?"

"Happy birthday, sweetheart!"

She bit on her lip. Natasha had made it a habit to show up every week without being invited and always at times that didn't suit Vivien at all. "Don't you wanna have your present?" her friend screamed through the intercom.

Vivien pushed the buzzer and a little later watched her friend sinking onto the kitchen bench, her fat bottom taking over most of it. She couldn't understand why Natasha had been letting herself go. She'd had the body of a ballet dancer when they first met.

Natasha said, "You eat regularly?"

"Certainly." Her appetite came in spasms nowadays, like yesterday at Hermannplatz, when she suddenly felt the urge to buy a *currywurst*, although she and Bernd had been vegetarians for decades. Then again, a whole day could pass and she would only realize in the evening that she hadn't eaten anything.

"How's Bernd?"

"Getting better each day."

Natasha took a small package out of her knapsack and shoved it over the table. "Happy birthday, dear."

Vivien opened Natasha's gift, saying, "We received a letter from the house management." She unfolded a table cloth and hung it over the chair, next to the dish towel. "Thank you."

"You can return it if you don't like it," Natasha said. "I saved the receipt."

"I like it," Vivien said, although they'd never used table cloths before and she wasn't planning to do so in the future. "We have to buy or move out."

"In my house they are letting two-room apartments," Natasha said. "There's a lift. And a balcony."

Vivien could feel her left eyelid twitching. Before, she'd thought that you couldn't see it, but she'd checked last time in the mirror – it had been visible enough. "Bernd would kill me."

Natasha smiled and then she suddenly put her hand on Vivien's hand. "Sometimes you gotta let go."

Vivien pulled her hand away. "We won't move, and that's the end of it."

"Do you still visit every day?"

"Of course I do." She would have to ask the nurse later. That would suit Natasha, to go and see Bernd behind her back. She got up and said. "Tea?"

Natasha nodded. "I found a nice book club. We meet once a week." She tapped on Vivien's book. "We read that, too. Why don't you join?"

Vivien poured boiling water on the tea bag and took it out only seconds later. She placed the hot cup in front of Natasha and said, "We ran out of sugar."

"Do you have milk?"

"Ran out of that too."

Natasha put her arthritic fingers around the cup. "Everybody's extremely nice," she said. "And you like to read, don't you?"

143

Vivien checked her own hands. Apart from the brown spots they looked okay. "I don't have time."

Natasha looked around. Soon she would bring up how often they'd sat here with friends, having dinner, talking and drinking until sunrise. And that it was time to do it again. She brought her gaze back to Vivien, let out one of her exaggerated sighs, said, "Are you coming to Yolanda's funeral?"

Vivien got up. "I don't do funerals." She reached for her plate, threw the remains of the sandwich into the trash, and put the plate back onto the table. How much time all this housecleaning business had consumed, hour after hour, every single day; and look at her now, she hadn't touched a broom or the vacuum in months, there was no need to fill or empty the dishwasher, just rinse a glass or a cup every couple of days, that was all. And the dust? Who cares about dust? Without her glasses she saw no dust.

Natasha smiled. "And the kids? Are they alright?"

"Kristin is coming on the weekend," Vivien said. "And Alexander's daughter already gained two pounds."

"Did you go see them? How are they?"

"Can't leave Bernd alone, can I?" Of course, she wouldn't tell her that Alexander had moved out of his girlfriend's place and that she had no clue where he was staying now. She'd offered him to come home, but he said that he couldn't leave town. She hoped that that was due to his new job. She hoped that he wasn't out of work again.

"What if I look after him while you're gone?"

Vivien grabbed Natasha's cup and said, "I have things to do."

She exhaled when she'd closed the door behind her friend's fat arse, called her son, talked to his mailbox. Although he hadn't finished his law studies he would know what to do.

They'd been living here for so long. They'd renovated every single room, they'd put in central heating, while everybody else was still using coal. Peter had helped, handsome Peter, who'd just turned fifty when he died of prostate cancer. He and Bernd also tiled the bathroom floor when Vivien was pregnant with Kristin, threatening to move into the first available new building, because with two toddlers she had the right to a decent place. "We never move out," she said to the mailbox before hanging up.

She opened the door and nearly fell over the neighbour's daughter who had been sitting in a pushchair not so long ago. Now she was sitting on the stairs, with mascara smeared all over her face and her eyes red from crying. Vivien said, "Are you all right?"

The girl shrugged.

"Can I do something for you?"

"Nobody can do nothing for me."

That's how far she got, being in tune with teenagers now. She bent down and put her hand on the girl's skinny forearm (anorexic?). "I guess I should tell you now that you'll soon be laughing again."

"All grownups say so."

"That's because they don't like to admit that they're terribly sad themselves."

The girl looked at her short nails, on which the green polish was chipping off. "Are you sad because your husband died?"

"He didn't die."

"My mum said so."

"It was just an accident," Vivien said. "He'll be home soon."

In the subway Vivien called Tom's son who was a realtor now. She told him that they could pay a hundred thousand

and he told her that no bank would give them the rest, considering their age and everything. "What do you mean by 'everything'?" she asked, remembering him playing with Kristin and Alexander when they were little. Remembering him moving in with them while his mom was in hospital and Tom had to work long hours. "I delivered my kids in that apartment," she said. "They can't kick us out like dogs."

When he wanted to know how Bernd was doing, she answered, "Fine."

She hurried past the reception. If she were asked what she dreaded most about this place she would choose the smell, but the reprints on the walls were the very next she would consider. The nurse with the henna-dyed curls approached her, carrying a tray. If only all these people would stop smiling.

"You're bringing the sunshine in, Mrs. Adamski," she said.

"How is he?"

"We had a restless night, dear."

"Give it a try with valerian." Vivien gazed at the yellow and pink sippy cups placed on the tray. "How is my husband?"

"The doctor wants to see you," the nurse said, still smiling. "He will be back in his office at half past three."

Vivien opened the door to Bernd's room. The second bed was still free. Her husband's roommate had died three days ago. His wife used to join her in the cafeteria, telling her how glad she was with all the children, grandchildren, nephews, and nieces coming by, but last time she'd suddenly said, "If I were in my husband's shoes I'd want somebody to shoot me." She'd brought her face closer, saying, "There are people who'd do it for five hundred."

146

Vivien bent over her pale husband, kissed his forehead, said, "They told me you didn't sleep well." She took off her coat and opened a window. Outside, crouched creatures were moving slowly, helped by canes or walking frames. Others sitting in wheelchairs were staring gloomily into the distance. Preferred clothing here was beige or pastel, with neither taste nor shape. Everybody gave the impression of expiring within the next twenty-four hours.

The first weeks she'd dressed Bernd in his favourite clothes, his and her favourite clothes, she'd made sure that he looked good, washed and styled his hair, covered his dead gaze with a new pair of sunglasses that she'd bought at the posh eyewear store on Oranienburger Strasse. Then, with the help of a nurse, she put him in a wheelchair and pushed him to the bench beneath the gigantic chestnut tree, where she fitted him with earphones, hoping that he would show any reaction if she played his favourite songs. She observed his face closely and excitedly noticed that his pupils were finally changing, but back home she checked the internet and found out that it must have been due to his medication.

Vivien put her head onto Bernd's shoulder. He'd been so strong, but now she could only feel his delicate bones. "We got a letter from the house management. They want us to buy the place."

She reached for his cold, lifeless hand, pressed it to her cheek, said, "Else we gotta move out." The sun was flooding the room. Before, spring had been her favourite season. Now, she could well do without it. She could well do without happy people sitting in the sun and pretty women wearing summer dresses and men rolling up their shirt sleeves.

"Your granddaughter is doing fine," Vivien said, taking the massage oil out of her bag. "She's already gained two pounds." She kneaded his fingers, one after another, then his palm. "Alexander sent pictures. She looks like him when he was little," she said. Once, she'd wanted to massage Bernd's back. The nurse helped her turning him around, but when he was lying there, like a corpse taken out of one of these gloomy Swedish thrillers, she got sick. She had to sit down and the nurse turned Bernd back to his usual position. The way she did it was so natural, without any effort at all, and Vivien realized that she was no longer the one who knew what her husband needed. She bent forward and whispered into his ear, "I feel so lonely without you."

She took his other hand and said, "Did I ever tell you that I was in love with Kristin's violin tutor?" Bernd continued staring at the ceiling, with that stupid grin distorting his handsome face. "The Russian guy, remember?" He'd always been so serious, sometimes slightly depressive, and now he was lying here, sneering like a preschooler snitching candy while his mum didn't watch. Vivien touched the corner of his mouth and pulled it down. "Roman was his name. I wanted to leave you. That's how much I loved him." She removed her finger and the corner went up again. "Never mind," she said and got up. "I was only kidding."

She took the iPod out of her bag. "No more special request shows," she said, scrolling the list until she found Tammy Wynette. Bernd loathed country music, especially sung by women. She pushed on play, observed his eyes, his mouth, nothing. She sang, "Our D-I-V-O-R-C-E becomes final today." Still nothing.

Dolly Parton was next. He continued grinning. She removed the earphones, turned off the iPod, said, "How could you do this to me?"

"Mrs. Adamski," the doctor said. "Take a seat."

Her gaze got caught by his running shoes. They were

the same ones she'd bought, only much bigger. She remembered how the sales clerk had tried to talk her into buying a 42 although she'd had a 39 throughout her life. She'd felt like a clown as she had to make some steps in front of him. When another customer interrupted them, she grabbed the smaller ones and fled to the cash desk. She sank onto the appointed chair. "When can I take him home?"

The doctor looked at some x-rays that were lying in front of him. "There's something we have to talk about."

Her tongue felt like glued to her palate. She whispered, "Can I have a glass of water, please?"

He reached for the bottle on the window sill and filled a glass. Tiny gas bubbles were whirling around as he put it in front of her. "We discovered ulcers in his intestine," he said.

Vivien felt the water run into her mouth. She felt the gas bubbles on her tongue. She drank up and said, "Can I have more?"

"A surgery would be a bit of a gamble." He refilled her glass. "In his state I would advise against it."

She stared at his coat. In between the second and the third button, there was a tiny brown spot. It looked exactly like the one in Bernd's right eye. Probably it was just a speck of lint. Probably the doctor would notice it as soon as he looked down on himself and he would flip it off, using his thumb and his index finger. But what if he'd spilled his lunch? Would he replace it with a freshly washed coat or would he try to remove the spot at the sink behind him? It was just a little spot, wouldn't it be a waste to put it in the washer because of that?

"Fortunately he doesn't feel anything," the doctor said.

"What do you mean?"

He smiled. "There's no pain."

She stood up. "What if he doesn't get surgery?"

149

The doctor shrugged. "It's your decision, of course." He held out his hand and said, "Sleep on it, and let me know tomorrow."

Back home she ignored the blinking light of the answering machine and walked through each room, looking at the framed photos. There were half a dozen of boxes filled to the brim with other frozen moments of their family life. She opened the cabinet and took out the bottle of wine that Bernd got from his department when he retired, the one they'd saved for a special occasion, and she put it on the table, and next to it, the corkscrew, and a glass. She sat on the sofa, the soon to be a hundred-year-old sofa that they'd bought from a friend for 50 marks at the beginning of her first pregnancy. They stepped into an upholstery when she was heavily pregnant with their second child and they looked at every colour in the catalogue, touched the fabrics, and finally went for velvet and *British racing green*; she remembered that catalogue, the many shades of green, she remembered how she fell in love with that name even though she actually preferred *avocado*. The sofa that cost them 2000 marks, a sum that made their hearts skip a beat in those days; she also clearly remembered the envelope they'd prepared, how they'd put it on the table, how thick it was, how Bernd said, "We could have bought a car for that, we could have bought two fucking cars." When the upholsterer and his assistant had gone, leaving behind their smell of sweat and sawdust, she lay down on the re-born sofa and pulled Bernd toward her and they made love and shortly afterward she felt the first contraction.

She opened the bottle. She hadn't had any wine since she and Bernd drank to their new grandchild, two days before she stood in front of the cheese counter at *Kaiser's* while he was getting a bottle of orange juice. When she heard the smashing of glass as the sales clerk was about to put the piece of Pecorino onto the scale, she said to herself that it was just a bottle that was smashed to pieces, which another sales clerk would remove shortly and of course they would pay for it, but her legs were moving as if she were a puppet on strings and she remembered thinking, "Slow down, your knees."

She filled the glass, brought it to her lips, took a timid sip. It didn't taste good. It didn't taste good enough to get drunk. She got up, took the glass and the bottle to the kitchen, and emptied both in the sink.

She was on her second round when a man passed her. The way he moved was regular, natural, without any effort at all. Not one of these overambitious guys training for a marathon. The ones who went by breathing heavily, the ones who'd consider themselves a failure if they didn't stick to their schedule. The man in front of her was clearly running for the joy of it, to feel his healthy body, his trustworthy legs, legs that would take him across town for hours if he wished so.

She ran faster until their legs moved simultaneously, until his rhythm became her rhythm, until she didn't need to fix her eyes on his muscular legs anymore, and she grinned, thinking of Doc Melzer's warning, and she rolled up her sleeves, letting the warm breeze caress her arms.

151

The Thing with Feathers

We need water for important things. It was here that we shared a bottle of sweet champagne after passing my mid-exams. It was here that we killed a six-pack of Beck's after granny died. And it was here that I told my brother Mika.

You must be kidding me, he said and May had only just begun but the grass was dry already and the straws pierced me through my T-shirt and I said, I don't want to go there on my own.

Mika took off his hat. He looked at it as if he were calculating the sum of the tiny squares. Then he said, Who was it?

Maybe I should have begun when you stepped on stage with your guitar and you looked lost and most of the guests were gone. Or maybe when you showed up next to me at the bar and ordered a beer. And another one for me. But I didn't tell my brother any of it, grabbed my stuff, and said, It's over there.

He didn't move. The water carried a plastic bottle past us and a mother duck and her ducklings were following close and I pulled at my brother's arm and said, Come on.

He said, Don't you have a best friend?

I hadn't told anybody. Never mind, I said, letting go of him.

He got up and walked to the bridge to get his bike. He wrapped the lock around his hips and said, Did you talk to the parents?

I shook my head. You'd understand if you knew them.

Jesus, my brother said.

Boats glided by and people lay in the sun and I heard them talking and laughing. I waited for Mika to ask about you again and maybe I would have told him that we walked along the deserted streets, you carrying your guitar, and that we listened to music in your tiny room, until I realized that I would be late for my poetry class with everybody waiting for my talk.

But Mika said, Why don't you ask the guy who got you into this mess?

I would have liked to tell him that my teacher looked at me and the students looked at me and I didn't remember anything I'd read in the uncountable books at *Staatsbibliothek*, just Emily Dickinson walking around in her garden.

But my brother would have said, Give it a rest.

We continued along the channel for a while and after another while we arrived at the house on Lausitzerstrasse and Mika locked his bike to a lamppost and said, What if they think that it was me?

An assistant sent us to the waiting area where several women with big bellies looked as if they would burst open any moment. Mika picked up one of the magazines and browsed through it. Then he put it back on the table and said, I booked us train tickets.

I said, Why?

He grinned and I shrugged and he asked if I'd forgotten our mother's birthday and I was happy about changing the subject. Mika picked up another magazine and said, Couldn't you be careful? Couldn't you just be careful, just for once?

And I remembered how certain I was that nothing had happened until the cross turned pink. Promise you say nothing at home, I said.

The last time we met you didn't say that you were leaving and I didn't ask why there were suitcases in the hall. When you took me to the subway in the morning I turned around once more and you stood there again like that first night, looking lost, and around us there were all the people going to work.

Mika put his arm around me and said, Who is it? I'll beat the shit out of him.

The other women smiled.

I remembered how we sneaked out of the house at night to take our bikes to the beach, when we were kids, my brother and I. It was just us and the wind and the moon. We were like newborn turtles, hurrying toward the water, by instinct.

Are you sure? Mika said and I said, How are things in the lab?

He let go of me and reached into the inner pocket of his jacket for his tobacco. "Ask again when I'm on Nobel's list."

One woman after the other got up and moved toward the doctor's room as if they had rheumatism. Some were going grey. Some were followed by men. Mika started rolling a cigarette. I watched a movie about Townes van Zandt yesterday, he said.

You said that it wasn't going well with the music. That the few gigs here and there barely paid your rent.

Mika said, His son's our age. He licked the paper, rolled again, and put the cigarette behind his ear. He listens to his father's records when he goes to sleep.

Mika started rolling another cigarette and then unrolled it again and shoved the tobacco back into his pocket. Musicians, he said. Always on the run. Always walking along some deserted street with their instrument.

Soon I would be sitting on the sofa and Mom would bring me a cup of tea and I would browse through old TV guides, regretting that I missed good movies.

Mika said, You're okay?

154

When are we going?

Friday.

I leaned back but made sure that my hand wasn't on my belly. I didn't want to look like the other women.

Then I had to wait in a narrow hall. Opposite to photographs of naked babies. Next to which there was a name and a date and a time and something like, Introducing, or Hello World!

Mika said, How's college?

I met you eleven times. I checked my filofax. How about having a falafel later? I said. My treat.

Mika took out his cell and put it back into his rucksack. Back to the papers and books filled with numbers and columns and calculations. Suzanne's waiting for me, he said.

Suzanne has a similar rucksack. Everything's predictable there. That's okay, I said. I'd throw it all up anyway.

What week?

What do you care?

He stood up and walked to the window and opened it. Look, a cherry tree.

Once I came by in the afternoon and you were standing at the open window too but it was February and the branches of the tree in front of your house were bare and you swept up the snow from your windowsill and formed a snowball.

Mika's hand reappeared with a bunch of blossoms and he said, They trained mice to fear the smell of cherry blossoms and they passed it on to their children and grandchildren.

They landed on my lap and I dumped them in the trash. Then a door was opened. What's that noise? I said.

Mika laughed. How many times did your heart beat since you were born?

One blossom stuck to my palm.

Math exam first semester, Mika said. Most forgot that foetal heartbeats are about twice as fast as ours.

I wiped my hand clean on my skirt.

In the end I stood in the room with the chair. I was glad that I wasn't alone but it had been a while since Mika and I undressed in front of each other. He turned around, looked at the books on the shelf, took one out, and laughed.

What is it?

Poetry.

I heard the doctor speaking to somebody on the phone in the next room. The first time I was here he asked me about my studies while examining me. There were many photographs of his own children on his desk but he was nice, even after I'd told him.

Mika was still standing there holding the book.

Read to me, I said.

He looked up. What?

Please.

When he was done I took off my skirt and discovered the blossom: the soft pink of the petals and the dark red spot in the middle, out of which tiny hairs with orange heads were reaching out for me, like the tentacles of a snail.

Care, Responsibility, Respect, Knowledge

For Tamás

He was at the second apartment around noon. His first cleaning job had been at a private place on Schönhauser Allee, with a piano, so he'd stayed longer than planned. But there was plenty of time; the new guests weren't coming before three thirty. And the former ones had left the place in a good shape: at least the kitchen/living-room looked immaculate. It was funny really; they paid for a cleaning service but felt obliged to do it themselves – these must have wiped the floor even! Karl checked the bathroom: clean and shiny too. He could as well lie down on the sofa, watch TV, doze off a bit.

The fridge was filled to the brim; he took out an unopened packet of eggs, a piece of bacon, orange juice. He put the frying pan on the stove and reached for an egg, absentmindedly gazing at the metal-coloured fridge that mirrored a girl who was observing him. He turned around and dropped the egg; she was standing in the doorway to the bedroom, dressed in a Barbie nightgown. "What the fuck?"

She stood there like a statue. Not a girl anymore, he'd say, with these large boobs and the face of a woman. A mongoloid! He said, "What are you doing here?"

She held up her nightgown.

"Holy fuck. Did you wet the bed?" He walked past her, into the bedroom she'd come from, and felt the mattress. "Shit." He pulled down the blanket, the sheets, everything. There was a huge stain; even if he cleaned it with all the soap he had here and turned the mattress around, it would probably smell of urine. He ran to the bathroom to get Chlorox, and the girl was still standing there with her hand

157

pressed to her crotch, but he would deal with it later, now the main thing was the mattress. There was plenty of time, he tried to calm himself down, plenty of time.

He opened the window, poured half of the bottle over the stain, rubbed until his hands hurt. Then he picked up the linen and carried it past the intruder, suppressing the urge to push her nose in, like he'd seen a friend teaching his Labrador puppy a lesson. "See what you've done? Didn't they give you a nappy?"

The girl smiled and then pulled the nightgown over her head. Beneath, she was naked! "Oh my God," Karl said but the girl continued to smile and passed him the crumpled cloth. "Don't," he said, then shrugged, then headed on to stuff everything into the washing machine. The girl followed him to the bathroom and grabbed a wash cloth and climbed into the bathtub.

"Hey," Karl said. "Get out of there."

She turned on the water. He turned it off again. "Listen. I don't know what you're doing here but we need to get you out. What's your name?"

Call the police. Call the police right now! They'll know what to do. But then they'd found out about Airbnb, right? This could get the boss into serious shit. The boss and him, if they came to ask why he'd been cleaning here in the first place. He couldn't possibly risk it. "Did they leave you here? Did Mommy forget to take you with her? Or Daddy?" What kind of parents would do that, even to a downie? They must have gotten used to her by now.

She turned the water on, drenched the washcloth, and held it up to Karl. "No fucking way," he said. He ran to the kitchen/living-room and grabbed his cell phone. Why should he deal with it? He was just the fucking cleaner, let the boss do it. The boss didn't answer. "Answer your fucking phone," Karl yelled when the mailbox turned on.

"I'm in real trouble here. Call me back ASAP, do you understand? Holy shit." He tossed his cell onto the sofa and returned to the bathroom. The downie was still sitting in the bathtub, holding up the cloth. He'd just read in some news online that one of them was starting a teaching career, they couldn't be that stupid. "Didn't they show you how to do it? Hey, really." He took the washcloth, put soap on it, pressed it into her hand. "Up and down, see?" He showed her the movements on his clothes, but she didn't get it. She sat there shivering, accusingly pointing the dripping washcloth at him.

"Okay," he said. "We'll do it together." He reached for her hand, pulled the washcloth over it, started with the legs. "What am I doing here? What am I fucking doing here?" He led the cloth over her hips and her stomach. He turned the water off and said, "That's enough now. Out!"

She stood up, looked at him with her thin arms slung around her shivering body, waited.

He grabbed a huge towel and put it around her. She still didn't move so he started rubbing her. "It's a dream," he said. "This all is just a fucking nightmare, I'll wake up in a minute and have a good laugh."

She dropped the towel and walked to the bedroom where she positioned herself next to the chair on which there were clothes, hers obviously. Someone must have put them there, they were neatly folded, washed even, he could smell the softener, fortunately also on the underwear similar to the ones his six-year-old niece wore. "Your parents did a lousy job. It's what parents do, teach their kids how to get dressed." He unfolded the undershirt. "You do have a Mommy, do you? A Daddy? Where are they?"

She raised her arms. If not for her breasts and the face, she could go for six as well. Maybe she was a midget too. Was that even possible? Weren't both genetic diseases?

Fucking unfair, he'd say. He pulled the undershirt down her body, keeping away as far as possible from her skin, and then reached for the underpants and held them up to her. "Come on. It's not that difficult."

She sat down on the chair, dangled her legs. "Halleluiah," Karl said. "A dream. Just a fucking dream." His gaze fixed to a Chagall print – identical to the one his grandmother had in her room at the old age home – he pulled the underpants over her feet, her legs, and when she'd jumped up again, over her hips. "Is that the way you do it at home?" He unfolded the sweater: Paddington Bear sitting on a leather suitcase. And that pathetic note around his neck: *Please look after this bear.*

Karl finished dressing her, tied her shoelaces, led her along the hall. "Listen, I can't keep you here." He opened the door. "I'm sorry." He wanted to pull her out of the apartment but she pressed her back to the wall and it was as if she was glued to it, he couldn't drag her away. He didn't use full strength of course, but he clearly signalled to her that he wanted her out, so why the hell wouldn't she listen?

He closed the door again. There was this chick he was seeing from time to time. Girls do this instinctively. Maternal stuff etc. They liked taking care of others. Because he fucking didn't. He left the stubborn visitor where she was, called the chick who was visibly irritated and brusquely answered, no, she was at university, couldn't possibly leave now, what about meeting for a couple of beers next weekend?

He looked at the other girl who had silently slipped into the kitchen/living-room and sat at the table now. "Don't move! Don't you fucking move until I figure out what to do." He sat down next to her, studied her face. "Do you understand me?" He'd thought that they were able to speak.

160

Not in the proper way of course, but they should be able to utter some sounds, shouldn't they?

"You're German, aren't you?" How could she possibly not speak? She didn't look like those who were totally messed-up. It was just the eyes really, the rest was pretty in a way. Like if she closed them you wouldn't even notice. "*Svenska?*" He rattled through all the foreign words he knew, observing her closely. When he came to French, her whole face turned into a smile. "*Comment t'appelle-tu? Moi, je suis Karl. Comme Charles, n'est-ce pas?*"

She started to laugh. How can that be that they suddenly become so happy about nothing? He fetched his cell to google "Down syndrome". So it was normal to be tiny, average IQ 50, identifiable during pregnancy. Why the hell didn't they get rid of her then instead of leaving her in this fucking apartment when it was his fucking turn to clean it? "How old are you?" He held up his hands and said, "I'm thirty-three." He opened and closed them three times, then held up three fingers. "Thirty-three. What about you?"

She laughed again.

"Didn't you learn that in kindergarten?" He reached for her wrists, raised her hands, said, "Ten, eleven, twelve, thirteen." She was still looking at him with that radiant smile, her shining strange eyes, as if he were the magician that mommy had invited to her birthday party. "Twenty-four, twenty-five, twenty-six?" Still no reaction. "Ninety-seven, ninety-eight, ninety-nine, hundred?"

The tiny hands suddenly showed a life of their own, she pulled them away and clapped. "A hundred? Nobody gets a hundred, you'd be fucking dead now." He returned to Wikipedia. Some lost the ability to speak at the age of 30. He looked at her face again. Maybe that's what happened. But she should at least understand him, it was written here. "What am I supposed to do with you?"

161

She turned her head. Karl followed her gaze. "You're hungry?" He reached for the cereal package. "It's empty. That's the only thing your parents forgot to buy." He stood up and opened the fridge. "Listen, I'll cook us something and afterward I'll bring you to the police. They'll find Mommy and Daddy. They're experts in finding people."

But first he had to clean up the egg he'd dropped and he also had to think of making the bed, really, what would the guests say if they came here and first thing they saw was that gigantic stain of piss. It wasn't anymore, of course, but that's what comes to your mind when you see a stain on a mattress, right? He turned around. Would she do it again? "Hey," he said, "Do you need to go to the bathroom?" Maybe they went more often than normal people, but why wasn't she wearing diapers then? He took the girl by the hand. "First wee-wee, then din-din." He laughed out loud. "What the fuck am I saying?"

The girl's hand was warm and delicate, holding on to him as if he was her fucking daddy. What would she do if he was one of the bad guys? Would she follow him around as well? What if he took her to the bedroom instead? Would she even try to fight him off? There were enough perverts out there, maybe they'd find it extra exciting.

"Come on," he said, pulling her to the bathroom. He shoved her inside, closed the door from the outside, went back to the kitchen, and finally cleaned up the floor. Then he lit the stove, poured oil into the pan, fried the bacon, cracked the other eggs. When the pan was steaming on the table, he returned to the bathroom. "You're done?" He waited, then said, "Lunch is ready." He waited, then carefully opened the door: the girl was standing right behind it. "What's the matter?" He stepped inside and pointed to the toilet. "Don't tell me that you don't know how to do this? What the fuck did they teach you?"

162

She stepped forward.

"You want me to stay here? All right. But hurry up now. Our food will be cold soon. I hate cold eggs."

The girl didn't move.

"Holy shit," he said, opening the lid. Then he pulled up her skirt, pulled down her underpants, sat her on the toilet seat. "Quick now." He listened to her pee, unrolled some toilet paper, pressed it into her tiny hand. "Either you do it or we leave that part out." He waited for a few seconds, then took her off the seat and pulled up her underpants. "They didn't have toilet paper in the middle ages. You won't die."

She followed him to the table and sat down. He filled her plate and then he filled his own plate and said, "Bon appétit." He greedily shoved the now cold egg into his mouth while she continued watching him. "You don't like it? You don't like eggs? I don't believe it." He took her fork, picked up a bit, held it up to her. "Yummy."

She obediently opened her mouth, chewed, and swallowed. Can that be true? Do you have to feed them? Will they be like that until the day they die? The doctors surely must have warned her parents, how could they do that to themselves voluntarily? He grabbed his plate, sat down next to her, took turns shoving the fork into his or her mouth. When they were done, he reached for a paper napkin and wiped her face. "What about dessert? Let's have a look what's in here."

There was yoghurt and ice-cream. He put both on the table and said, "What would you like?" He opened the yoghurt, she didn't object, he fed her, she finished. "Okay, then I'll take the ice-cream." Her eyes followed his every movement. "You wanna have a try?" This time she opened her mouth double and she opened it again before he'd even had the chance to refill the spoon. "How can such a tiny person eat so much? Where does it go?" He fed her until

163

she leaned back in her chair and he wiped her mouth again and the clock said that they had one hour and a half. He browsed over the last paragraphs on his smartphone: 92% went for an abortion.

"Stay here," he said. "I have to work now." So this was the plan: he would get everything ready, take her to the nearest police station, come back, hand over the key, and charge his boss fucking double. He went to the bedroom and felt the mattress: it was far from dry, but if he turned it around it would do. Most important, that reek of piss had gone. He opened the dresser where the bed linen was stored. It was empty. "Shit. Really, this fucking arsehole." He called his boss again, let off steam on the mailbox, browsed through his contacts. Whom could he call for help? What could he say? "Get that downie out of here? Bring fresh blankets? Pinch me, make me wake up from this fucking nightmare?"

There wasn't enough time to take the subway to Alexanderplatz. He couldn't think of any nearer place and wouldn't he hate to spend his last money on fucking sheets? The other apartment, the one where he'd played the piano this morning, they had plenty of linen, a whole antique chest full of it. And the place was ten minutes away.

"All right," he said to the girl. "You stay here. I'll soon be back. Don't touch anything, okay?" He grabbed his coat. "Don't fucking move."

The girl stood up and reached for his hand.

"No," he said.

Again she suddenly developed an incredible force. He wasn't able to retrieve his hand, at least not without hurting her. "I warn you, we'll have to run. This is no happy after-school stroll, do you understand?" He dragged her out of the apartment, down the stairs, along Kastanienallee. He pulled his hood over his head and said, "Aren't you cold?"

164

She was just wearing her short skirt and that pathetic Paddington Bear sweater. He sighed and took off his coat. It was much too big for her, nearly reached her feet, but at least she'd stopped shivering. "Your parents should go to prison for this, really." He pulled up the zipper and said, "Mommy and Daddy are very, very mean. How could they leave you alone?"

Or maybe they didn't. Maybe something happened to them. But what? Where? In the apartment? Let's assume, let's *just* assume that they were murdered, a) wouldn't there have been at least a trace of a fight? Blood? And b) why would somebody break in and murder them? There was nothing in that place except for furniture and a TV. Which was still there. It made no sense. So they must have left the apartment, maybe to go shopping. And then? Why didn't they return? People don't get abducted here. It was their last day, they had to leave, the only possible answer was that they forgot her here, really, how can you forget your fucking child?

He pulled her into the house that he'd left only a couple of hours ago, and how he'd left it, in such good spirits after playing the piano for at least an hour, he hadn't touched one since he came to Berlin, how could that be anyway, he needed to find somebody with a piano, he didn't realize how much he was missing it. He pulled her up the stairs and into the apartment and only then did she loosen her iron grip.

"Stay here." He hurried to the bedroom, opened the chest, reached for two sets of linen, a couple of sheets. There was no bag here, so he went to the kitchen to get one and when he returned, the girl had disappeared, there was just his coat lying on the floor. "Hey," he cried out, "where the fuck are you?" He searched in the children's room first, then in the dining room, then in the living-room and there

165

she was, sitting in front of the piano. "We're done here. Let's go."

She raised her hands and let them fall on the keys with all force.

"Hey!" He tried to lift her from the chair but she'd locked her feet around the legs. "Do you want to have a beating? You're a nasty child, aren't you?"

She raised her hands again, only now she didn't attack the keys, but slowly led her index finger from left to right.

He held her by the wrists and said, "Okay, I'll show you how it's done and then we go, all right?"

After a while she untangled her feet and allowed him to lift her. When he sat down on the chair, she climbed onto his lap. "No," he said, trying to get rid of her but she quickly locked her feet around his own legs now. "You're really something, aren't you? Must have driven your parents insane, that's why they're not here anymore. Surely they had to be taken to the loony bin."

He touched the keys. "So what is it you wanna hear?" Wasn't Mozart good for kids? Something light anyhow, not too depressive, he remembered Wikipedia mentioning a tendency toward depression. No surprise really. He started playing sonata No. 13, which seemed to please the little brat enormously. She swayed back and forth on his lap – arrhythmically of course, he had trouble staying in rhythm himself – and started humming – so she was able to produce sounds! Then she put her hands on his and strangely enough he was able to continue playing.

Like a kid she was, really, he felt her warm body, maybe it wasn't so bad in the end, maybe you get used to anything after a while, maybe you begin to accept the weirdest things, like having a downie who can't talk and doesn't even know how to use fucking toilet paper. "That's Mozart. Wolfgang Amadeus Mozart. Ever heard of him?"

She leaned her head against his chest and sighed.

"You like that, don't you?" He played the Turkish March next, which made her jump up and down on his lap, then he abruptly stopped and slid from the seat, and this time he'd surprised her, it was too late to lock her feet around anything. He pulled her to the hall, wrapped her up in his coat, and took her back to the apartment, where the clock above the sink was threateningly ticking and the bed was still unmade.

"I'll tidy up here, you watch TV, all right?" He made her sit down on the sofa and browsed through the channels until he found a cartoon. Then he put the clean sheets on the bed, unloaded the washing machine, cleared the table, noticed a pen, a pen and a notepad. Of course, that's how they did it: when she wasn't able to speak anymore they made her write it down. He went to the sofa, sat next to her, put the pen and the notepad on the coffee table. "Look," he said, "Maybe we won't have to go to the police after all." What could they do really? They didn't have downie experts there. He reached for the pen, wrote down his cell number. "That's how you can reach me." Then he gently put the pen between her thumb and index finger. "Now it's your turn." He held her hand over the notepad. He waited. Finally he felt a movement. It was clearly her, he wasn't doing anything. Maybe they had at least thought of that, teach her to remember a fucking cell number, to make her memorize it, so that someone could at least fucking call them. Once he'd run into a little boy at the grocer's, he was crying, had lost his mother, on Christmas Eve, when everybody thought of shopping like five minutes before closing time, but this boy at least knew his mother's number, it was amazing really, he rattled it down like a poem. "Let's call Mommy and Daddy, okay?" How could he have been so stupid, he'd read that they all went to a

167

normal school nowadays, they were mixed with normal pupils, weren't they? They taught them how to write, that's what schools are for, teach them kids to write, doesn't matter if they're normal or a downie or have to sit in a fucking wheelchair.

He made his hand light as a feather, closed his eyes, stopped breathing: He felt her hand going up and down, left and right. "Go on. You're doing fine." He waited until she stopped moving and then opened his eyes again. She'd drawn the sun. And the moon. And the stars. "I wonder who will pick up if I dial that," Karl said.

She looked at him. If it weren't for the eyes, really, he wouldn't be able to tell. And it was not that he didn't like them. Fucking honest eyes, he'd say. Like, these eyes wouldn't tell no lie to nobody. A little sad maybe, but with that smile on her face, who knows. He gently pulled the pen out of her right hand, reached for the piece of paper, discovered the word in the upper left corner. It was hardly decipherable but eventually he was sure that it couldn't mean anything but LEYLA. "Is that your name? Leyla? Gosh, that's beautiful. Are you an Arabic princess?" Of course not, with that fair hair. "So what is your father the sheikh paying when I return you? A million? Two million?" She laughed and he said, "Five million euros? Wouldn't that be awesome, Leyla?" He looked her in the eye and smiled. "So that'll be my last cleaning job I assume. Let me finish it properly then."

Without a warning she threw her arms around his neck. He stopped breathing, his heart pounded against his chest. Her arms hung on to his neck, and the only thing he could do was put his arms around her too and they sat there until she decided to let go of him again and when she did, he said, "Right. Let's do that now."

He was cleaning the dishes when the doorbell rang.

"Holy shit," he whispered. They were early. No fucking way that they were early. He had to hide her, but where?

Karl turned off the TV, lifted the girl, carried her to the bathroom. "You stay here, don't move. If you move, the monsters will come and they will eat you alive, you understand?" He shut the door, threw a last glance over the place, and then went to the front door and opened it. A woman in her fifties stormed in. A man her age, supposedly her husband, followed suit and behind him, there was a guy of maybe twenty, whose face was the image of guilty conscience. "I'll kill you if something happened to her, you stupid moron!" the man hissed.

"She's here," the woman shouted and the rest of the family joined her and Karl stood in the hall, waiting for them to finally address him, apologize at least, explain to him how all this had been possible, but they didn't even turn around, and neither did the girl who reached for the man's hand, while the other guy was hugging her, crying like a fucking baby. Eventually they led her out and the woman looked at Karl as if she only now realized his presence. "Who are you?"

"The cleaner."

She turned around and ran out. The door downstairs fell into the lock with a big bang.

Karl looked around for a few moments as quiet settled around him. Then he went back to the sink, added hot water, and reached for a dirty plate.

169

Shooting for the Moon

I hadn't seen Marina in a couple of weeks, and of course I didn't expect a miracle – or maybe that's what I'd hoped for anyway – but I'd become an expert in pretending: I kissed the air next to her cheek, holding my breath, making sure not to come too near to her translucent skin. "How are you?"

"I missed you," she said.

I had told her that my aunt needed her house cleaned up before moving to the retirement home. My brother was taking care of that, though. I'd spent the time spying on my boyfriend and the bitch he was fucking. "Any news?"

"There's a new patient. He's twenty-nine."

"Is he cute?"

"Very." She smiled. "I lied about my age."

"He wouldn't believe you anyway." Every time I visited she was getting younger. She'd reached her mid-twenties by now. All the wrinkles were gone. I gave her the incredibly expensive scarf I'd bought at Gallery Lafayette and said, "That's just perfect with your eyes. Exactly the same colour."

She unfolded it. "It's real silk, isn't it?"

"Guess so."

She turned the scarf around, as if she didn't know what to do with it, as if she'd never worn one, and yet that's what she'd been doing for the last two months, wrapping a scarf around her head. By now her closet was full of them; she could choose one in the morning like my father used to choose a tie when getting ready for work. "You shouldn't have spent so much money."

I attached the speakers to my iPod, turned it on. "Remember Cookies?" It had taken me quite a while to find the CD we would listen to before partying. I'd searched in

170

the cellar, in my daughter's room, I asked all my friends. They didn't even remember. It was a compilation by a DJ who stood behind the turntables at Cookies. "Too loud?" I turned the volume down. "We're going to dress you up tonight. I want to take some pictures for the family album."

"Pictures?"

I smiled. "Yeah. Pictures of my beautiful friend. We better do that now, we won't get any younger."

"I remember that song," she said.

"Gotta prove to them kids how cool we were."

I removed the lunch tray that she'd hardly touched to make space for my make-up bag, went to the bathroom, put some of Marina's facial soap on a washcloth. The shelf was bursting with anti-aging lotions and masks guaranteeing to take away 84% of wrinkles, stuff I needed much more than her now. I looked at the mirror, checking if my smile didn't look too artificial, returned to her, said, "Remember when you had that fling with the DJ?"

"At Cookies?"

"The DJ at WMF." I gently led the washcloth over her face. "Don't you remember? First, you told the barman at Pip's to come back after he was finished for the night. Then we went to Cookies, and you got sick on the hood of the Porsche."

"What Porsche?"

"It was parked in front of the entrance." I took out the foundation I'd bought for her in the afternoon, after realizing that mine would be much too dark. "Gosh, the owner freaked out."

"I don't remember," Marina said.

"He filled you up with vodka-lemon." I touched her cheeks lightly with the rouge brush, rubbed it off again – she looked like a clown – and said, "After you got sick on his Porsche, we had to carry you home."

171

She chuckled. "Did he stay?"

"He was happy to get away without having his Armani suit wrecked." I had a look at various eye shadows and finally went for a light aubergine. With skin that pale you had to be careful. Then I took the false lashes out of the bag and said, "Hold still."

She drew back. "Not these."

"I'll be careful, I promise." I gently put some glue onto her upper lids. "Beauty knows no pain." Pressing the lashes on her lids, I said, "I perfectly remember that night."

"Do you?"

"First, you thought that you would have to stay home because your mum had the flu, but then she felt better, so we took Leonie over to be with her." It was her daughter who'd given me the fake lashes. She'd bought them for a party but her friends convinced her that her real ones were already too much to handle. "Look at you!"

Marina opened her eyes.

"Like Marlene Dietrich. Honestly." I took the kohl and drew a line where her brows had been. "You'd hardly stepped onto the dance floor when the DJ jumped off the stage and grabbed you. He took you in his arms and whirled you around as if the fucking dance floor was just for the two of you. Everybody was staring at you, like they would be staring at Cinderella and the prince. It was weird really."

She laughed. "I didn't lose a shoe, did I?"

"You'd rather lost that prince, honey. We'd just bought them, don't you remember? With heals that high!" I quickly took off her old scarf and wrapped the new one around her head. I'd checked the internet to find out how it is done and practiced on my son, who was wearing his hair very short now, yet it was another story if there was no hair at all. But in the end, she looked like an Egyptian queen. And I'd been right; the colour matched her eyes perfectly.

"And?" she said.

"After five minutes you took off." I reached into my bag. "Guess what I've got here."

"Tell me."

I let her peak into it. "Well?"

"I don't believe it," she whispered.

"Don't ask how long we've been looking for it." I took the jumpsuit out of my bag now, the one she had worn that night. Black velvet, with a décolleté that just took your breath away. It had been her mum's idea to look into the boxes they'd stored in the attic after clearing Marina's apartment.

She pushed away her blanket and slowly sat up. "You think it still fits?"

"Sure. A model would be jealous of you now." Even though her mother had warned me I had been taken aback because she'd lost so much weight. "You left and went to the hostel around the corner."

"There was this workshop. All the DJs were staying at that hostel." She slowly got up, walked to the window, looked out. We were on the 20th floor; the sky was closer to us than the town. She pressed her front against the glass and said, "I remember that room. We were lying on a bunk bed, the top one, and you could see the TV tower from the window and it looked like a space shuttle. We were pretending to be on the moon. Then his roommate came in, but he just said, 'Don't worry about him. He lives in another time zone. He's still sitting in the bar getting pissed."

I chuckled. "He was lying to you."

"What?"

"Time passes quicker down here."

She turned around. "What was his name?"

"How would I know?"

"I forgot his name."

173

I put my arm around her. "You never remembered names, honey," I said. "There were too many." In the beginning, when she was still up most of the time, we were sitting on the windowsill for hours, and every sentence began thus: "Remember the guy who…" But we wouldn't talk about the ex-husband who brought a bunch of roses every other day, and we wouldn't talk about the boyfriend who was cheating on me. I smiled and said, "We were always shooting for the moon, weren't we?"

I helped her put on the jumpsuit. She looked like the plumber who had fixed our new sink the previous day, but I had thought of bringing safety pins. "That's how they do it with super models," I said. "You look gorgeous, honey."

She looked down at herself. "You think so?"

I went outside to find one of the nurses. And to give my mouth some rest. The nurse who used to play scrabble with Marina looked up from the desk.

"Is there a room with a large mirror anywhere here?" I asked. "Not for myself," I added quickly, "for Marina."

"There's a gym on the second floor," she said and walked me back to Marina's room. "Jesus, you look beautiful," the nurse said as she poked her head in.

Marina slipped into her Havaianas.

"Where are your shoes?"

"I only brought my sneakers."

I succeeded in pulling my mouth's corners higher. "I'll be right back."

In the corridors I only met patients in slippers and people working here wearing plastic crocs. Nothing interesting in the lobby either. I could have taken the bus to the next shoe shop but I didn't want to leave Marina alone that long, so I went to the cafeteria, ordered an espresso, waited for a miracle. When the waitress brought the check, I asked her if she happened to have a pair of high heels.

"Yes," she said.

I still can't believe that I'd asked her which size they were. But I must have because I still can hear her saying, "Thirty-nine, but they feel larger."

"That's perfect," I said.

Marina was lying on her bed again. I showed her my prey. "What do you think?" I said.

"Sexy," she whispered.

I put them on her feet and rearranged the scarf. "You rest for a while, and then we'll start."

"Ever heard of Kübler-Ross?" she said.

I lifted her head to put a towel beneath it. "You don't want to ruin that pillow with your lipstick."

An hour later she was still sleeping. It was dark already and the city had turned into a sea of lights. I was blinded by the thousands and thousands of windows behind which people were doing the things they were always doing, ordinary, meaningless things like filling the dishwasher, drinking a glass of water, listening to the radio. They would be doing those things another day and another and another. And here was Marina, lying in the hospital bed that had become much too big for her. I carefully removed the safety-pins, adjusted the silk scarf, kissed off her lipstick.

Then I took the shoes back to the waitress.

175

Acknowledgments

These stories wouldn't exist without the help of many others. Patrick Calvert and Bill Kouwenhoven looked closely and patiently for spelling and grammar mistakes. *Mick & Keith, Rome, A Place to Be* and *Floating* were discussed during workshops given by Alexi Zentner, Josh Weil, and Benjamin Percy at Sierra Nevada College, and my fellow students carefully read and commented upon them; I'm still keeping their notes in my treasure chest. Alexi 'forced' me to write *Stains, Last Planet* and *All Invisible from Where We Stand*. Randa Jarrar inspired and helped me with *Tell Me About France* and encouraged me to write crazier and longer. Gayle Brandeis reminded me that my job is and was to listen, to console, and to give hope.

My children, Lilli, Helena, and Giora Falzoi, have always been very supportive and encouraging; they made sure that I wasn't disturbed while sitting at my desk, they accepted that they have to share me with so many other people who weren't even real, and now that they are grown-up, they've become my first critics whose honest comments helped to improve this collection.

But most of all I have to thank Philipp Marouschek, who was the first one to call me a writer and whose thorough and sincere feedback turned my clumsy first drafts into real stories, who inspired me, who took care that I finally had a room of my own to write in, and who made it possible for me to study creative writing in the US. There wouldn't be any publication without him.

Other Publications by Bridge House

Links

by Dianne Stadhams

LINKS – sometimes random, many times unplanned, often with far reaching consequences, always shaping our journey from cradle to grave – the stuff of life.

Just how do Atta Gatta the child-eating crocodile, Scheherazade the pantomime star and Judy the stammering Goth strategically connect characters across the globe?

Enjoy this trilogy of inter-linked short stories that will make you smile and squirm as they raise questions about the needs and challenges of our contemporary world.

Order from Amazon:

Paperback: ISBN 978-1-907335-63-1
eBook: ISBN 978-1-907335-64-8

The Art of Losing

by Paul Williams

In this internationally-acclaimed collection of contemporary literary fiction stories by Paul Williams we are invited to appreciate what it means to master the art of losing – to let go of things both big and small – whether it be dreams, or love, or houses, or whole continents. Told with wit, humour and pathos, the stories reveal the unexpected narratives that often flow beneath the surface of contemporary lives.

The twenty stories lurch from continent to continent across Australia, Europe and South Africa, from child to teen to adult, from past to present, from war to peace, from me to you.

Order from Amazon:

Paperback: ISBN 978-1-907335-61-7
eBook: ISBN 978-1-907335-52-5

Keepsake

by Jenny Palmer

Keepsake and Other Stories is an anthology of short stories by one of the growing number of brave women writers. Jenny Palmer brings us stories of otherness, witchcraft and magic close to home and further afield within Europe. We meet all sorts of characters: those who rely on guard dogs, those who shun social media and those who are obsessed. We even meet a Neanderthal man. There are paranormal stories, a story of bad neighbours, and a story of redundancy. And many more. All to be enjoyed.

"Jenny is totally in control of her stories. They are memorable and perfectly crafted." (*Amazon*)

Order from Amazon:

Paperback: ISBN 978-1-907335-57-0
eBook: ISBN 978-1-907335-58-7

www.ingramcontent.com/pod-product-compliance
Lightning Source LLC
Chambersburg PA
CBHW051516170626
46811CB00002B/847